I0676994

Escaping Time

Angela H. Distrola

Copyright © 2015 by Angela H. Distrola

All rights reserved. Printed in the United States of America. No part of this book may be used or reproduced in any manner whatsoever without written permission except in the case of brief quotations em- bodied in critical articles or reviews.

This book is a work of fiction. Names, characters, businesses, organiza- tions, places, events and incidents either are the product of the author's imagination or are used fictitiously. Any resemblance to actual persons, living or dead, events, or locales is entirely coincidental.

For information contact : www.angiehdistrola.com

Book design by Distrola Designs

Cover by SelfPubBookCovers.com/FrinaArt

Author Photo by Martin Studio (www.tommartinstudio.com)

ISBN-13 : 978-0692483640

ISBN-10 : 0692483640

First Print Edition: July 2015 © Distrola Publishing

10 9 8 7 6 5 4 3 2 1

DEDICATION

I would like to dedicate this book to my loving husband. He puts
up with my craziness every day, and when I   told him about my
idea for this book he told me I should write it. After a year of
saying I'll get around to it he finally made me sit down and write it.
So thank you for believing in me and pushing me to get the story
that was in my mind out. Now I just need to get the next two out
of my head and on paper.

ACKNOWLEDGMENTS

Thanks to my friends Kim, Liz, and Cody, who when they heard I was writing a book gave me encouragement when they told me they would love to read it.

ESCAPING TIME

Book one of

Through the Veil Series.

Time. Everyone knows there are sixty seconds in a minute, sixty minutes in an hour, twenty four hours in a day, seven days in a week, four or five weeks in a month, twelve months in a year, and three hundred and sixty five days in a year. This is the accepted norm. No one questions it. Have you ever stopped and asked yourself why that is?

People fight over everything. The smallest things, from religion, politics and sports, to what type of cell phone is most popular, or which form of government is better. We as a people even fight over which style of pizza is better, deep dish or thin crust. The topic doesn't matter, you can choose any topic big or small and we as a people will find a way to fight about it. We all have different views. We all have different theories. Whether we believe in them ourselves, or if someone else believes in them, the issue is irrelevant.

It is in our nature to fight, but then why is it that no one fights about the concept of time? No one debates if it's real or not. Time is the one thing that everyone agrees on. Doesn't that seem a little strange to you that there is only one thing in this world that no one questions? Have you ever even stopped to think that time wasn't real? That there were no limits to our life span? No, probably not. As you have been embedded with that information from the moment you were conceived. You probably haven't ever questioned the existence of time. Have you ever stopped to think why that is? Why no one questions if time is real?

Well, what if I told you that time doesn't exist. Would you believe me? What if I told you it holds no meaning and just the concept of believing that it exists will be your own undoing. If you believe in time you are trapped in an endless cycle, which you most likely will never leave. So let me start with my journey and maybe I can help you to break through the clutches of time.

Chapter One

I was 18 years old. Again time has no meaning but for your understanding I will use your terminology so that you can see from where I started. That being said...

My name is Rosalie White. I was just an average girl living an average life. I grew up in a small town in Eureka, South Dakota, where the crime rate is low, we have good schools, and no traffic congestion. We have a beautiful lake and park area which allows for a variety of sports opportunities. I just finished my senior year at Bawdle High School, Class of 2005. I was getting ready for my four years in college at Dakota Wesleyan University.

Everyone kept telling me I need to get my head in the game. I need to figure out what I want to do with my life. I shouldn't waste my time. We only have so much time to figure out what our purpose is. Why are we here? We need to make our time on this earth count.

Well I just didn't know what to tell them. So I just nodded my head and told everyone I understood and agreed with them. I replied by saying I'm weighing my options. When in reality I had nada, zip, and zilch. I was just trying to bide my time to come up with something, anything tangible to tell them. Well, I had nothing, not one clue. I mean really how do you pick just one thing? You need to devote so much time and effort into becoming good at something. If you want to be truly good at anything it takes years of hard work to do anything well.

Take becoming a Doctor. You have to go to pre-med for four years, then four years for medical school, and three years of residency. All that studying and all those exams! Even after that you still have even more training before you are truly on your own. For what? One day having the chance to make a tiny mistake and cost someone their life? Umm no, that's not for me. That's just too much pressure for me I wouldn't be able to handle the fate of other people's lives in my hands.

Really that's just too much to put on someone. Doctor, I guess that's out! Ok so how about a lawyer? Same thing lots of time studying. Also having to pass the bar just to practice law. For the same effect. If you don't file the right paperwork or even better miss a deadline, and a criminal walks free! So what do I want to spend the rest of my life doing?

I decided I had enough with the unpacking. My two best friends and I had just moved into our new apartment. We were excited to start our adult lives together in our downtown apartment. I was happy that my apartment was only a few blocks away from my parents' home. It was far enough away for independence, but I could easily walk there if I got home sick. Well I had been doing enough unpacking the last couple of days. We had just moved into our apartment just off campus to get into the 'we are adults gear'.

I just needed to get out and think some life choices through. I couldn't stand to empty one more box or put one more book on the shelf. I had so much on my mind. I just needed to get out of the box filled apartment and clear my head of all the decisions that still needed answers.

I took one last look in my mirror. All this stress over these life choices was bound to give me wrinkles. I put some moisturizer on my fair skin, silently wishing I had perfectly tanned skin to go along with my long brown hair and light brown eyes. After I put some eyeliner on I ran a brush through my long brown hair, while taking a deep breath in and letting it out slowly. I shook my head when all the decisions came rushing back to me like a tidal wave.

This pressure was making me feel trapped with the walls closing in on me, which is why I couldn't stand to be inside a minute longer. So that was when I had decided to go the park. I really just needed to think about a few things. Well, my main question what am I going to major in? What do I want to do with the rest of my life?

Those were the questions I was struggling over when I saw him. He was the hottest guy I'd ever seen. Light brown hair, blue eyes, and a body that looked as if it had been chiseled by the best artist in the world. He was just standing next to the water fountain in the middle of Oak Hill Park.

I had come here to do some quiet life reflecting, and also to procrastinate from unpacking. I was in the downtown park quietly weighing my options of what classes I should be signing up for. I mean, what else should I sign up for other than the core class that the school demands that I take like Math, English, and another language that they deem necessary for all freshman to take.

I mean really like life isn't hard enough at this point they have to throw in these core classes. Which I might add that you have to pass to move on to the classes you came there for. I mean really, didn't we just finish all this crap in high school? I might add that I get distracted easily and change topics quite frequently. You will see what I'm talking about here very soon, I'm sure. But anyways, as I was saying before I went off on my tangent.

He was just standing there looking, no, the word that I'm looking for is observing. Yes observing. Yes, observing, that better describes what was happening. He was observing this old couple holding each other's hands sitting really close, across from the bench I had picked to do my quiet self-reflecting, and just enjoy the beautiful summer day that was before us.

At first I thought he was admiring the cute old couple. As I often enjoyed watching those select couples, who even after decades of being together are still in love. In love and completely happy spending life's little moments with each other. I mean really, to spend so much time with one person and not end up resenting or hating them after thirty or forty years together, it brings me hope that someday I will find that once in a lifetime kind of love. Sorry back to the hot hunky guy that started my tangent. So after a minute of watching him watch the old couple I saw how he was looking at them.

He was not watching with the adoration that I would have expected. He had a look of pity, mixed with maybe disgust. When I saw that, I got so mad my body just got up without permission from my brain. May I say that tends to happen quite often. I mean my mouth, yep it most definitely has a mind of its own most of the time. Well I got up, and with a purposeful stride went right over to him and blurted out

"What the hell is your problem?"

At that moment my brain slowly clicked into place and I realized I was no longer sitting on my bench, and my brain was like

"Ahhh, hell"

Chapter Two

He turned to face me but he had this startled look on his face. Maybe it was more confusion than startled, I wasn't exactly sure. Then he proceeded to look around him as if I were shouting at someone behind him. When he realized I was actually talking to him he started off with saying.

"I'm sorry do you mean me?"

I have this thing about stupid questions. They just send me over the deep end. So I snapped.

"Ugh, well yeah ass hole who the fuck else would I be talking to?"

Ok if you haven't picked up just yet I tend to swear a lot! Sorry, tangent again. At that moment he started to grin at me like I had just made this hilarious joke. I had this strange feeling in the pit of my stomach that I couldn't put my finger on.

If he wasn't so drop dead gorgeous at that moment, with the sun hitting his light brown hair and illuminating his face, I swear my story would have a completely different ending, because I would have dropped his grinning ass on the fucking ground and gave him a piece of my mind. Instead my brain actually took over for my mouth for once and drew a complete blank. Thinking back to it now it was those damn blue eyes they just drew me in and wouldn't let me go.

As I was standing there with my mouth gaping open, he took that moment of my silence to with a cocky grin I might add, said.

"Hi I'm sorry for the confusion my name is Christian, and I'm sorry but I didn't understand your initial question. What was it again?"

I wasn't sure if it was the haze that suddenly came over me or what, but I had this weird feeling in my stomach that I still couldn't understand. Finally my brain released my mouth and I blurted out,

"What the hell is your

problem?"

"What problem do you think I have?"

He raised his eyebrow at me, and his smile curled into a smirk.

Oh do I hate when people answer a question with yet another question. So in retrospect I might have come off a little bitchier than I initially intended, but man what the hell? Does this guy really want me to kick his ass or what?

"Oh, I don't know. I don't understand how someone can have such a look of disgust when looking at an adorable couple. A couple who have obviously been together for such a long time. I mean these days having a successful marriage last more than a decade is a rarity. People don't want to put the effort in to make something great."

I was exasperated.

"Oh yes I understand what you mean now. I'm sorry for the confusion."

He replied.

"Ok, well then, why don't you enlighten me?"

I said after it was obvious he wasn't going to proceed.

He just stood there giving me this questionable look. He had his head tilted to the side and was biting his lower lip as if he was forcibly trying to hold something back. I could tell he was in deep thought but finally after about a minute of just standing there in silence, I just caved and said.

"Well I'm waiting. Would you enlighten me with your wonderful explanation? The one to why you could have such horrible emotions going through you when you are looking at this absolutely adorable couple sitting right there?"

As I pointed to the couple that was sitting on the bench. I looked over to realize they were no longer there. So I started looking around wondering where they might have gone.

Chapter Three

I had the strange feeling in the pit of my stomach again. I just couldn't shake that feeling. As I was thinking to myself, wondering why I had such a weird feeling building up in my stomach, I got that feeling that you get when someone is watching you. So I turned back to Christian. Who I might add had that cocky grin on his face. So I snapped.

"What? Why are you giving me that look? Oh and where the hell did that cute old couple go? They were just there a second ago. I'm sorry but old people don't move that fast. I swear they were just there! But hey please enlighten me to why or how you could have such a down right horrible response to a nice couple who enjoy spending their time with each other?"

So finally he answered me.

"I have no ill feelings towards the

couple for loving each other. Love is such a wonderful thing. It is the best part of our worlds. It is what creates such wonderful things."

"So what is your problem pray tell? I mean you were giving them such a hateful look did they do something to you then?"

"No they did not."

He replied

"So?"

I prompted him again, and waited for him to answer me.

"So I don't have an answer that you could fully grasp. I'm sorry what was your name? I didn't ask you before."

Christian replied as he gently caressed his index finger over his bottom lip, as if he was in deep thought about something.

"Oh, I'm sorry, my name is Rosalie"

I stopped and blushed a second before his outlandish question of me not being able to understand his response came flooding back into the forefront of my thoughts.

"What do you mean I couldn't fully grasp? Do you think I'm dumb or something?"

I shouted back at him.

"No Rosalie. Might I add, that is a lovely name for a lovely girl such as yourself."

He said as he was giving me a look of curiosity. I would have wondered what he was thinking, but he had this way of angering me.

"Well thanks, but flattery will not help you out with accusing me of not being able to grasp your concept. I mean what the hell is your problem? You can't just give me a simple answer to my question? You have to disregard my question with yet another question, then just tell me I'm too dumb to understand!"

I felt my blood start to boil.

"No, no Rosalie, I'm afraid we started off completely wrong. Please let me assure you I do not think of you as dumb. I was just trying to convey my explanation to you. Your initial question is that of something I do not think you would believe. Therefore you would not fully understand my answer."

He shrugged his shoulders at me like it was a simple statement.

"What do you mean I wouldn't believe?"

I couldn't believe this guy, what the hell was his problem?

"Well Rosalie let me try to explain. I'll start by answering your previous question."

"That question was?"

I interrupted, I was a little flushed with the fury which was emulating from every pore in my face.

"Well, Rosalie you asked me where that couple went."

Christian replied.

"Oh yeah."

I took a deep breath, and some of the tension left my body. I continued on.

"Where did they go? They were just right here a minute ago, and we've only been talking for a couple of minute's right? And I'm sorry but old people can't move that fast. Not to be mean or anything. There slow."

I took a deep breath then continued.

"So where did they go? Did you see them leave? Did they leave because you and I were shouting and disrupting their peaceful moment?"

I retorted.

"The couple well, how should I explain this without you over reacting?"

He looked at me and raised one of his eyebrows at me.

"Over reacting?"

I shouted maybe just a little too loud.

"Yes. I wouldn't want to frighten you or upset you."

He said in a reassuring voice.

"Frighten me? What the hell do I look like bub? A little girl? How could you upset me? Could you just get to the point please?"

I snapped getting frustrated again. Man what is this guy's problem? It's not like it's a hard question, really just spit it out already.

"Well if that's what you would prefer. I guess I could just come right out and say it."

He said with a reluctant tone.

"Yes please Christian. I'm getting old waiting for you to just spit it out already!"

"That's it right there Rosalie you're not getting any older."

Christian remarked, frustrated he ran his hands threw his hair.

"Ok Christian I'm starting to really lose my patience. Get to the fucking point!"

I shouted as I started to fidget from side to side.

"Well Rosalie the older couple, they were on the bench but when you came up to me and started a conversation you unintentionally left that moment with me."

He remarked with a scholarly tone.

"What do you mean left that moment?"

I said with a hint of confusion in my tone.

"Well you would call it a moment in time."

Christian replied with a cute smile that spread all the way up. His eyes had an excited twinkle to them that seemed to dance in the light of the sun.

Chapter Four

F inaly, I found my voice again, after staring into his eyes with the allure that they held within, I said.

"Moment in time? What are you saying? We've traveled to a different point in time? You're saying we time traveled?"

At that moment I thought he'd lost all his marbles. Or maybe there were cobwebs in his noggin, but then he cut off my minds babbling and responded with.

"No, not time travel. We left the concept of 'time' altogether. You see you still believe in the concept of time. Therefore..."

And that's where I cut him off.

"Concept of time? What nonsense are you about to spew?"

I giggled rolling my eyes at him.

"Please, Rosalie I know this is hard for you but you asked, could you..."

"Hard for me? What the hell? Did you forget to take your meds or something? Are you tripping off acid or something? Or perhaps did you escape from the mental institution down on 24th and Wayne street?"

"No could you please just let me explain without interrupting me maybe?"

Christian jumped in with an exasperated look on his face. Which might I add looks goddamn awesome on his wonderful body!

"Rosalie, Rosalie"

Christian called

"Oh sorry sometimes my brain just takes off on me. Yes I will let you explain."

I said even though I still thought he was crazy. Hot but crazy. I thought smirking to myself.

"Thank you. So as I was saying, you still believe in the concept of time. And with those beliefs you are unable to fully understand the world or shall I say worlds we live in. Before you jump in and ask, yes, worlds. Well technically, we all live in the same world but just on different planes, I guess, that is what you would call them."

"I'm sorry, Christian. I've got to stop you right there. So you mean to tell me when I came up to you, you took me to a different plane of existence?"

I raised my eyebrows in surprise.

"Well, kind of. Rosalie, the reason I was so shocked when you started to talk to me was I was just observing your plane. I wasn't within your plane. So you shouldn't have been able to see me. No one else has before. Let me try to explain as your people explain it; you use only a certain percentage of your brain. Thus, you don't tap into the full capacity of your mind. My people believe..."

"Wait... sorry, I know I'm interrupting, but please what do you mean 'your people'?"

"Sorry Rosalie well there are others like myself just as there are others like you. I promise I will get to that ok?"

"Yes sorry, Christian, go on."

I said

"So, my people believe when the belief of time became stronger, the brain sectioned itself off unable to co-exist with the magic in the world."

"Magic? Christian, really?"

I said as I'm sure I was giving him a very questionable look. Ok maybe the nut house was on the right track. I thought to myself.

"Rosalie, would you like to see?"

He chimed in with that cocky smile I was starting to enjoy.

"See?"

I questioned.

"What do you have to show me? Can you pull a rabbit out of a hat?"

I started giggling and that's when my world shattered. Everything that I had known. Poof disappeared. All the times that Emily, Paige, and I watched movies about magic, with wands and chanting spells. All the hocus pocus, and all that shit. All of that paled in comparison.

In the movies they always had to do this big ordeal before they got any result, like saying this big long chant that always had a rhythmic timing to it, and they used potions that took forever to brew, just to get this 'poof' for an explosion that turned a frog into a prince. Or there was a wand that they had to wave in just the right way accompanied by the right words, to get a feather to hover slightly above the table.

Bam! All of that just came to a halt. As I was thinking he was downright crazy, and making plans to find a cop to take him back to the loony bin. I looked at his right hand, and I swear I almost shit my pants. My whole perspective changed. In front of me, what I thought was an awesomely hot guy who I perceived to be legally insane, proved me wrong. Perhaps, I was the delusional one? His hand was stretched out, palm side up, hovering above his hand was a ball of fire. I lost it.

Chapter Five

"Oh my god, oh my god. Your hand is on fire."

I screamed, and as I was about to tackle him to the ground to extinguish his hand, he flicked his wrists and the flames turned into the most beautiful thing I think I've ever seen in my whole life.

They looked to be like tiny diamonds dancing around until they took the shape of a beautiful rose. I think I stood there for like ten minutes with my mouth completely touching the floor. The tiny diamond like things just floated there. Shimmering and twinkling in the afternoon light. I swear I could have lived in that moment for the rest of my life. How could this be possible? Never in my wildest dreams had I ever even begun to contemplate that magic was real.

How could there be a completely

different world so different than my own? As my brain was working around the possibility that maybe magic was real and I had traveled into a different reality or realm, or whatever Christian had called it, I started to think that maybe his crazy had rubbed off on me or something. Wait is crazy contagious? I hadn't thought that it was possible to catch crazy. I stood there, for I don't even know how long as I contemplated the realm of possibilities about somehow his crazy delusions rubbing off on me, that I hadn't realized that I was lost in the endless babbling of my mind. Until in the calmest voice ever he said.

"As I was saying, I was just observing your plane when I saw the old couple and you came over to me. When you entered my conversation, you apparently crossed over into my plane. That is why I was, confused as you shouldn't have even been able to see me. Our planes don't normally cross. Well at least not yours to mine. I can freely view your realm as I please."

"How, how d-did you do that?"

I stuttered like a five year old who doesn't know what point they want to get out.

"Do what, Rosalie? The fire, or the stars?" Christian retorted with a cocky grin spread across his handsome face.

"Any of it? How did you do that?

I stammered, completely in awe.

"Well, Rosalie it's simple. All you have to do is to believe, then you can do anything and..."

He opened his hands and a large bouquet of long stem white roses appeared out of nowhere. He handed me the stunning array of flowers and said.

"Would you like to know more my dear?"

That's how it all started. With just one instantaneous moment of going to confront a stranger, all because I couldn't believe he could give that sweet old couple anything but an admiring look. Who would have ever thought that they would be given the key to such great knowledge while procrastinating about figuring out what they want to do for the rest of their life?

I mean really, I've procrastinated about a lot of

things in my life: Science projects, Math homework, studying for that really big test that all the teachers are saying is the hardest test they've ever come up with. I am great at procrastinating. Probably because my mind switches topics so easily.

I mean once I was telling my mom how I got awesome news from my English teacher about my college application essays, and I had suddenly remembered that she had told me this hilarious story about this girl forgetting to turn in her essays, and tried to break in to the admissions office. When it brought back a memory that once I ran into our counselor at the school when I was turning in my admissions essay for my college applications, and spilled her coffee all over her new dress. The principal saw the whole thing and spewed coffee outta her nose.

Aww that was great. Coffee was everywhere. My mom just sat there staring at me shaking her head saying Rosalie your college essay? What did your English teacher say? You started to ramble on about other stuff before you told me the news your English teacher told you.

Like I said, I'm great at switching topics, procrastinating and speaking my mind. Up till now it's only ever gotten me in trouble. So this was kind of new for me.

Chapter Six

H e started by telling me that,
"Long ago there were these great men who believed life was lacking. They believed they needed to create an order to life. They gathered together trying to come up with something to balance the world and the people who resided with in it. At first all seemed well. They decided to use the sun and the moon to create this order. By calling the sun 'day', and the moon 'night'. Now if you didn't know this, when you give something a name, you give it power. Just like believing in something you are giving it power or creating magic. The more you believe or the harder you wish the stronger the magic."

He stopped only to take a deep breath.

"Once they created day and night they went further, creating hours, minutes, and seconds, giving them certain properties. Such as so many seconds create a minute and so many minutes create, an hour. So many hours in a day and night. This made the power strong. Now, you may not believe this to be a mistake, but like I said giving something a name creates power. That's exactly what they did. They gave power to their new creation by calling it 'time'."

I think he paused for a dramatic effect.

"Unbeknown to these great men they had created something that withheld such great power. There creation 'time' had so many shall we call them, 'rules'? Yes, rules. Sixty seconds makes a minute. Sixty minutes makes an hour. Twelve hours was a day and twelve hours was a night. After they decided on days and nights, they went even further. They wanted to break up the different kinds of weather."

Christian took a deep breath before he went on.

"So, they created the word 'seasons'. And within those seasons they created months. And after months, they made up years.

Tying all of them together by giving the years so many days. The more they relied on their creation, the stronger the magic of time became."

He shrugged his shoulders at me.

"All was well for a while. People started to believe that it made their life easier to have this 'time'. They went on with their lives using the new invention relying on it with every breath they took- and with everything they did. More and more people took on this concept of time, working it into their lives so completely that they hadn't even noticed when it had started to take over."

He paused his speech, as he raised his hands motioning that time had taken over everything around us.

"The wise men began to forget the old ways. At first this didn't seem to be such a big deal. They went on with their lives, embracing their new creation. With each passing of their days, they forgot more and more of what use to be. They created devices to help them hold their 'time', such as hour glasses and sun dials so they could see their masterpiece."

His face saddened with this part of his story.

"The men were so happy with this new invention, or way of life, they didn't notice that they weren't using their magic as much. They showed others their inventions and told them how it worked. Soon others had these devices that helped them hold their time too. When they decided that 'time' could be kept, that's when they sealed their fate. Their creation took over, splitting us in to two realms."

He shook his head at the thought.

"Time was all they could see. As their time passed, they started saying they didn't have enough time. There wasn't enough time in the day. They had forgotten about magic, the way it worked and how to wield it. The magic within their creation of 'time' heard them, even though they didn't know how to use it. 'Time' seemed to control the magic of those who believed in it. So it created the very thing they had said: not enough 'time'."

He took a deep breath in once again and continued.

"They had forgotten that they had created this thing in which they were stuck within. It was as if they had forgotten they themselves had given the guidelines to their rules of 'time'. It became as if they were trapped in one of their hourglasses. We could see into their realm but they could no longer see us. The more they said they didn't have enough 'time', the more they truly believed it."

I could see the hurt in his eyes. There was a deep pain just under the surface, dulling the beautiful blue eyes that had me in a trance.

"As I said, you only have to think it or believe it and so mote it be. After a while we could see that their bodies had started to change, they looked wearier. We believed it was because they had started to believe they didn't have enough 'time'. They came to a belief that there was a beginning and end of 'time'. They called this change 'aging'. Again, giving it a name created its power. The men and women started to age even faster."

He paused momentarily as if it was hard for him to talk about.

"With their aging bodies it proved to them they were losing time. As this happened, they started to believe there was an end to 'time'. As they aged, they believed life had to start from somewhere thus they came up with the word 'birth'."

"Wait, wait, wait are you telling me you don't age?"

I interjected. I hadn't seen that coming.

"No, Rosalie I do not believe in the magic of 'time' therefore it has no hold on me."

Christian stated sounding frustrated with me.

"WHAT!"

I stammered. I swear I must have looked hilarious with my eyes bulging out of my head. My mouth dropped to the ground, but all he did was smile at me and continue on with his retelling of the beginning of 'time'.

Chapter Seven

"The men and women became so obsessed with their aging bodies, they started to believe there was a point in which time ended, and a point when it begins. A point in which they could no longer go on. As this belief started to take hold, some of the people started to die."

He looked down at the ground like he couldn't look me in the eyes.

"With the proof that life had a limit to it, the people started contemplating how long they had. Trying to figure out how many years they had left. It became a frenzy. Everyone was worried that their 'time' was coming to an end."

He was shaking his head with disapproval.

"Those who believed so strongly

that their 'time' was near, the sicker they got, proving to themselves that there 'time' was almost up. Now that there was an ending to 'time' there had to be a beginning. As the old died the young couples found themselves with child. Or as you call it pregnant. The cycle of life began. With each death there was life born."

His eyes widened slightly.

"With their 'time' ending they got frantic. They set out trying to find ways to expand their lives. With each of their passing generations, the magic of 'time' got stronger and stronger. Their realm got further and further away from ours."

He looked so sad. I just wanted to reach out and comfort him.

"The people had used their magic less and less. No one knew that 'time' was created by magic. They didn't know what it had been like before. Magic was almost unheard of. Only a select few even attempted to use it. Even those select few didn't understand how to use it completely, or how they knew about it at all. They believed it to just be an old tale passed down through the years. Until they had forgotten about its existence almost completely."

Shaking his head in disapproval.

"Some had created stories about magic, but none thought it to be real. They didn't truly believe in it, therefore unable to use it. It was Just a story to pass their 'time'. Some created rituals and they believed they would work but only the truest believers could get the magic to work for them. Even the truest believers had limitations to the magic they could wield. If only they knew, if they could just stop their belief in 'time', they could have all the magic they could dream of."

"So, Christian, you're saying if I stopped believing in time I could do magic?"

I asked with a look of suspicion.

"Why do you have such a hard time believing me, Rosalie? Did you not see with your own two eyes the magic I showed you?"

He countered with a look of skepticism on his face.

It took me a moment. I was sifting through the story he had

just told me and yes, I had just seen him create a ball of fire in his hand. Along with thousands of diamonds shaped into a glorious rose. Oh not to mention the white bouquet of roses I still held in my now trembling hand. Why was it such a hard concept to grasp? I had just witnessed it as he stated. So why is it so inconceivably hard to believe? At that moment I had made a decision. I wasn't going to doubt him.

Chapter Eight

"**O**k, Christian"
  I said.

"I believe wise men decided to create 'time' and doing so forgot how to wield magic, but if you don't believe in 'time' where do you come from? If you do not age or grow old what happens to you? Do you die? Were you born?"

I was starting to get a plethora of questions piling up in my mind when he finally cut off my internal thoughts. It was as if I was seeing a marble swirling and swirling down a spiral drain. You know like those things you put a penny in and watch it go around and around and around. You get my point. I felt like I was in the twilight zone. Nothing made sense to me. If 'time' doesn't exist what would that mean? Is up still up and down still down? Is there such a thing as up and down? What about gravity?

Is that real or is it made up too?

Oh my god. There are so many questions. What questions do I need to ask? What are the most important questions? I started to feel as if the world was spinning faster and faster. The gravity started to get heavier and heavier. It was getting harder and harder to breathe. I think I took less oxygen in with each passing breath.

Till finally, I felt a strong warm hand touch my shoulder. There was a spark. As if I was statically charged. You know when someone who is wearing big fluffy socks drags their feet along the carpet and touches you, kind of shock. So back to what I was saying. He led me to a bench. Well, I thought it must be a bench as we were in a park after all. Then I heard his voice. His strong deep voice that seemed like music to my ears. He was telling me to breath, take slow breaths in and out, in and out.

When I finally came to my senses, or what was left of them I might add. I saw the haze that had taken over my vision start to resend. The ringing that had started to take over my hearing started to go away. When I finally looked up, I saw only his face. He had a look of concern on his face as if something had gone seriously wrong. Though before I could ask him what was wrong I got a sense of my surroundings. We were no longer in the park. We were in a small room with furnishings that of a living room or waiting room of some sorts. I was completely confused. We had just been in the park standing there talking about 'time' not existing and yes, I remember getting dizzy but I didn't lose consciousness, did I? So how had we gotten here?

Chapter Nine

"Christian, where are we, and how did we get here? Why do you have that look on you face? What's wrong?"

I asked.

"I'm sorry, Rosalie, I didn't mean for that to happen. I didn't know telling you about all this could have affected you the way that it did. I'm so sorry"

Christian replied.

I looked up at him, and saw he genuinely was worried about me. Even though we had just met, he was truly frightened. Scared that there was something wrong with me. Even though I had been screaming and yelling at him. Accusing him of being crazy. He was kind enough to be concerned for my well-being.

I was gazing into those deep blue eyes. The eyes that seemed to go on and on forever. When I saw him smile. This was different from that cocky grin that he had given me before. It was soft, gentle, but it seemed to go on for miles and miles. I sat back in the chair that he had helped me into. When I did, I got a better look at his entire face. The look he was giving me made my heart skip a beat. My breath caught in my chest. The way his eyes were lit up, and the smile from ear to ear made me feel like a schoolgirl with her first crush when he finally looks at you from across the room and actually sees you. Noticing you for the first time.

I couldn't help the smile that spread across my face, or the flush that was slowly warming over my cheeks. In that moment, I knew that I would never want to leave his side. Just the way he made me feel. There was a part of me that was calling out for him. I knew it was something special. Something life altering.

Not to say that what he had just told me wasn't a life changer, but at that moment I knew my life wouldn't feel complete without him. It was as if my soul was trying to reach out and grab hold of him and never let him go. I had never thought something, or someone could make you feel so complete, so whole. As I sat there contemplating to myself how this man, this complete stranger, had made me feel, I finally I had worked up enough strength to speak.

"No, Christian, its ok I'm fine really. I just got overwhelmed with all the questions that I wanted to ask you, I swear I'm ok. Speaking of questions. Where are we? We were in the park before I sat down. Is that correct?"

"Yes Rosalie we were in the park but when it looked as if you might faint I brought you to a more suitable location to sit and talk. Was that ok? Did I do something wrong? Would you prefer to be back to a more familiar place such as the park? It's really no problem I can take us back there if you would prefer."

He said sounding worried.

"No Christian this is perfectly ok. You did nothing wrong. Thank you for your concern. I'm fine really I am. So where is here?"

I pointed to our surroundings, with the hand not holding the bouquet of roses.

I looked around more meticulously. There were several comfy looking chairs with a soft blue rug laying underneath them. You know those rugs that when you stand up in your bare feet you can't see your toes because there are devoured in the soft plethora that is complete and utter comfort. Oh how I love those carpets. I'm not one for wearing shoes. I know it is weird me being a girl and all. But I love being barefoot. Those carpets just feel like heaven on your bare feet.

Sorry, I jumped subjects. The chairs themselves had intricate patterns all over them. Each one with a slightly different pattern and corresponding colors that linked each one to the others. On one of the end tables was a beautiful vase, its beautiful pattern looked as if it had been made just for this room. The walls were painted a taupe. You know the color that could almost go with any décor. There were paintings all around the room. Some landscape's, others were portraits of young attractive looking adults. The one portrait had three men and three women, sitting on a beach enjoying what looks to be a picnic. If I had to guess their age

I'd have to say mid to late twenties no more than thirty.

The landscapes had beautiful depictions of all different scenes from all around the world. Waterfalls which I would have to say maybe from the tropics? Golden grasslands probably from the Midwest. Rolling hills from the east and oceans with blues and greens which were so vibrant it made you feel as if the wind was blowing the fresh sea air right in front of you.

Oh how I would love to have talent like that. To be able to make such fabulous works of art with nothing more than a brush, paint and a canvas.

Of course I wasn't given any talents that you could brag about to your friends. Or even make a decent living off of. I enjoyed pottery, but I really wasn't all that good. Funny enough not having any talents, is how I ended up in this very spot having these mental rambling. Ironic isn't it? Not knowing what I wanted to do with the rest of my life, led me to one of the greatest experiences that I would never have even dreamed about. Again Christian interrupted my mental babbling with saying.

"I brought you to my place. We are with in my, I guess you would call it living room?"

He raised his eyebrow in a silent question to me.

"Really this is your place? Wow for a guy your age having a place that's not floor to ceiling pizza boxes and beer cans is kind of impressive!"

I said with shear wonder spread across my face. I placed the bouquet of roses down on the coffee table beside me. As Christian suddenly shouted.

"Rosalie how often do I have to tell you 'time' doesn't hold meaning? I don't have an age."

I snapped my head back up and looked at him as he continued in a calmer voice. Looking remorseful for his outburst.

"How about this, we can try this a different way. You said before you had questions. How about you ask me your questions and I will try to explain them to the best of my capabilities! How does that sound? We could sit here or if you would prefer we could go to one of those places."

He pointed to the pictures that

hung all around the room.

"I saw how you were looking at them. If it would make you more comfortable or feel relaxed, I could take you anywhere you wish to go."

"Well as much as that sounds like fun here is ok with me for now."

I said

"All right then. Before we get started would you like anything to eat or drink?"

Christian asked.

"Well now that you mention it I guess I am a little hungry. Is there any where we could order lunch from around here?"

He gave me that cocky grin again. And said.

"Well Rosalie, no there isn't any place we could order from, but how about you tell me what you would like, anything at all. Even if it's from your favorite restaurant. Just tell me what it is and I'm sure I could whip it up for you!"

He smirked.

Oh Kay my momma told me if you ever find a guy that can cook grab him and never let him go!

Now if you find a guy that likes to cook marry him right on the spot no questions asked. I mean man who is this guy? He's tall has great looks, and genuinely cares about others. Now I find out that he's confident that he can make anything my heart desires. I might never leave.

"Umm well now I'm not sure. How about a calzone with extra ricotta and extra onions! Sauce on the side. Oh or maybe some pizza logs, or onion rings and a chocolate milkshake. What sounds good to you?"

I asked.

He had that cocky grin again, and that's when I knew he wasn't planning on going to the kitchen to make us some food. He started moving his hands in a circular motion. All of a sudden there before us was a table. On the table were calzones from my favorite Italian bistro, pizza logs from the pizza place down town, onion rings and a milkshake from my favorite fast food restaurant.

Again my mouth hit the floor, and my eyes were hanging outta their sockets. If he didn't stop doing this he would think I'm simple. Ok simple isn't exactly the

word. How's easily impressed?
Well I guess that will have to do
for now.

I turned to look at him and you
could just tell he was so pleased
with himself. Like I said he thinks
I impress easily. Well hey in my
defense the guy had just created a
table out of thin air in a different
realm and put all of my favorite
foods right there in front of me! So
yeah I guess he could take this
moment as impressed. I was
fucking awestruck. If he keeps this
up I might need to invest in a gym
membership or something. Oh well
what is a girl going to do? Me I'm
going to savor every last bite and
not worry about all the calories.

I'm going to tell myself that I
deserve every bit of it as I was just
told the truth about the universe
or whatever. My brain needs its
strength from something familiar
to prepare for what's to come. As
I'm sure there's going to be a lot
more of the insane to come.

Chapter Ten

So after I indulged on all my favorite foods. Hey don't judge me I know there was a lot of food ok. But after I finished I looked up to see him smiling at me.

So I asked him.

"What? Is there a problem? Do you think I'm disgusting because I just ate all of that food?"

"No, no. nothing like that my dear. It's just nice to see a girl with such a healthy appetite!"

"Well ok then. So how about we get to some of those questions then."

I said with a grin spreading across my face

"Yes Rosalie, what would you like to know?"

He relaxed further into his chair and crossed his right leg over his left. He looked so calm, so at peace. His smile started to grow when I realized I had been staring at him instead of asking him my questions. So I tried to stop thinking about how good he looked and how much I would like to crawl over to him and run my fingers through his thick light brown hair. Questions, questions what were all those questions I was just dying to know?

"Umm well"

I stammered what should I ask him first? He said they created 'time', birth, and death. He doesn't grow older. Umm this is going to be a long conversation.

"Ok how about we start with the whole birth and death thing! I mean you said after they started to die they got pregnant! So what are you trying to tell me? Were you not born or something crazy like that?"

"Yes that would be a good place to start. No Rosalie, I wasn't born. I was never a child as you say I don't change I am me and always have been since I was created. This is where we differ. I was created by magic."

He said matter of fact.

"We believe there was enough free forming magic left over from the creation of the universe, and we took our form from the remnants of that magic. I have always known everything that I know. I have no parents, I have always been me!"

He shrugs at me apologetically before continuing.

"You were born from parents that go back generations and generations leading all the way back to the beginning of 'time'. When the creators of 'time' started dying the others created birth. They believed they had to have come from somewhere so they created children. Think of how you procreate. Two people coming together and suddenly there is this tiny thing inside the woman! How do you think that possible? It's magic."

He shrugged at me.

"Oh my god you're telling me it's magic that created me?"

I was dumb founded.

"Well yes rose doesn't that make more sense?"

He asked me.

Ok I don't know why this is just

so much to take in. I told him I had an open mind and that I believed all of what he said, and god knows he's given me enough proof but wow this is everything I've known! How can I just stop believing what I know to be true and tell myself that none of it is real?

"Well I don't know if it makes more sense but continue please."

I motioned with my hand for him to go on.

"We believe as the souls of those whose bodies die they moved into their creations of birth"

I cut him off with my question.

"So reincarnation?"

I lifted my eyebrow at him.

"Again a name your people have given, but yes reincarnation as you would say. The old as you call them passed on, their life force moved on into the creations of life, or babies as you would say, they created. Does this help any? What were some of your other questions?"

He asked me calmly as he used his magic to make a mug appear in his hand. While he waited for me to come up with my questions he took a sip of the contents of his mug.

Ok no 'time', no birth, or death. When we die we are so to say 'reincarnated' into another body as a baby.

"Well I kind of have a follow up question relating to the whole death and birth aspect of your scenario."

I said as I bit my lower lip waiting for his reaction from my statement. He looked at me with an apprehensive look. Like I had just said something completely stupid.

"What else would you like to know about the subject then?"

He raised one of his eyebrows at me.

"What happed to the souls before they went into the babies' bodies? I mean there had to be 'time' or moments, while the babies were growing that the souls weren't in a body. Where were they? What did they do? Did they remember what happened while they were bodiless?"

I asked him shyly.

"They were there, they just had no form."

He shrugged.

"So they were like ghosts?"

I shrieked.

"Your people have given it many different names. Let me see I believe they've called them ghosts, or explained it as a place called limbo? Or Heaven, Hell. Many of your people have explained it in different ways. They have come up with many different terms for the state of being that they over take during that ordeal. Is that more helpful?"

He questioned.

Well that's interesting I guess in a way there is life after death. That's one question I've always had that's been answered for me.

Chapter Eleven

"What about the fact that there are so many people on earth now? I mean the population is always growing there isn't a set number of people in the world. Our people must be more than the original amount of people that changed their beliefs and started to believe in 'time'. So I guess what I'm saying is where did all the souls of the people that are living now come from? If the souls are as you say recycled than how do we have more people?"

I asked puzzled.

"Well they'er not!"

He said.

"What does that mean?"

I said confused.

"I guess I mean that not every one of those creations has a soul."

He shrugged at me with a wiry

look on his face. Like I was about to erupt at him at any moment. Which I might have but I think I did a pretty good job at controlling my complete and utter shock.

"So you're saying that not everyone on Earth has a soul? What does that mean for the people who don't have a soul? How are they alive if they don't have a soul?"

I questioned him.

"Well haven't you ever wondered how someone could kill or have no emotions? Why so many people are depressed and don't feel complete?"

He retorted.

"So a psychopathic killer doesn't have a soul?"

Well I guess that kind of makes all the sense in the world. I mean why would anyone do those things? There are a lot of fucked up people in the world, but man really having depression could mean that you don't have a soul? I think that's kind of crazy, isn't it?

"So what you are saying is that everyone who is depressed doesn't have a soul?"

I gawked at him.

"No, not entirely. Some people

might just be unhappy. But not all of those people have a soul. Some of my people think that at some point the souls of those who died, broke apart. Some people might have a fraction of a soul. We aren't entirely sure of all the specifics, but that seems the most likely scenario."

He said to me while I was trying to think about those who don't have a soul. How are they alive?

"So what does that mean for those people who don't have a soul?"

I asked him completely confused by this subject.

"Well, I guess you might say they'er empty inside? Or confused? I'm not quite sure how to answer that question. I have no personal experience that would allow me to give you that kind of information. What about you? How do you feel?"

He asked me.

I don't know how do I feel? How would I know if my soul is intact?

"How would I know if my soul is intact?"

I asked while I was worried that there was a possibility that my soul wasn't whole. That there might be a part of me that is missing.

"That is a good question. One I'm not entirely sure can be answered, but only you hold the answers to your life. I know I have shed some light on things that are literally out of your world, but I can't promise that I hold every answer that you might seek. I can only try to the best of my ability to answer the questions that I am sure you have many of."

He took a breath before he continued.

"So Rosalie what were some of your other questions that you had if you were finished with those pertaining to death and souls. Did I explain that well enough for you?"

He asked as he raised an eyebrow at me.

"I understand that you may not hold all the answers that have come to mind over this revolution. I think you are doing a wonderful job thus far with your explanations."

I said smiling at him.

Chapter Twelve

What else? "Gravity?" I squeaked feeling a little overwhelmed

"Ha-ha"

He belted out. I looked up and all of a sudden I was furious! My face was burning red and I just exploded

"What? Why is that so funny?"

I felt my face grow hot and I knew it was bright red.

He looked at me and his laughter just cut off. I swear he paled just a little bit when he registered the fury emanating off my body. He swallowed and took a long deep breath.

"I'm so sorry Rosalie, I've never had a conversation quite like this before. You just took me off guard. Please forgive my outburst. What about gravity?"

He said in a timid voice, like he was afraid of my wrath.

"Does it exist?"

I asked, as I talked using my hands to form my question.

"Well yes."

He stated shortly.

"Is that all I'm going to get from you? Just a simple yes? You tell me time isn't real it was created by magic, along with birth, aging, and death. Some people or should I say a lot of people don't have a soul or maybe broken fragments of a soul. What else do I believe in isn't real? I don't know what to ask. I'm at a loss, and I have to tell you for me to be speechless is quite a feat."

I was furious, and confused. There was just too much going through my head.

That one hundred watt smile was back on his face. His shoulders seemed to relax. He took a deep breath and continued.

"Well, your people tend to do a lot of things differently! When they forgot about magic and how to use it they had to learn do things differently."

He said matter of fact.

"How so?"

I asked puzzled by his statement.

"As I showed you we can create anything with magic. When they stopped using it even the simplest things like making food changed for them. They created jobs to fill their time. Everyone learned something different so they could get everything done. They had limitations because of their 'time'. So growing the food, picking, cleaning, and cooking, it was so much more work. We just think what we want to have and."

He waved his right hand in a circular motion around his opened left palm. Suddenly there was an apple just lying in his outstretched hand. Staring at him, I started to get what he was talking about. It takes forever for crops to grow, and then the 'time' it takes to pick and clean them all before we can eat them.

"So things don't need to grow?"

I asked confused.

"No not really, but you can. Let me show you."

He put down the apple next to my bouquet of roses. Then he

stood, and rotated his hands in a large circular motion. A fog or a mist appeared. It was swirling upwards going faster, and faster. He stopped swirling his hands and stepped back so I had a better view. As the fog or mist dissipated I saw a large blue planter, within it held a small tree. The tree had apples, oranges, and cherries on it.

"See we can grow just as you but we have no limitations as your people do. From where you come from they created science, and things have started to change. I've seen them create things that you probably think are quite amazing. Am I right?"

He gave me this probing look, as he awaited my answer.

Ok, yes I have heard that they've genetically created a fruit tree that can grow like three different types of apples, and at the time I was like no fricken way! But this is just unbelievable. Apples, oranges, and cherries. Let's see those scientists pull that one off.

"Ok yeah what else?"

I raised an eyebrow at him.

"Your   people   created

transportation. First they used horses, and then carriages, now you use cars, planes, trains, and boats. All to take you to some destination that they want to go."

He looked at me waiting for my response.

"Then how do you get around?" I asked puzzled once again.

"Would you like me to show you? It's easier to show you that to tell you. Trying to explain such simple things is very hard."

He gave me a shy smile.

"Well I think you're doing a great job so far."

I smile at him and bat my eyelashes.

"How would you explain what a tomato tasted like, if I told you I'd never had one?"

He asked raising his right eyebrow and smirking at me.

"Ok you've got me there. So how would you like to show me then?"

He stands and holds out his hand for me. I looked into his eyes. They were soft and reassuring, but they had a warm undercurrent to them like a spark of heat ready to jump out from excitement. I'm not quite sure which made me feel more ready but I put my hand in his and with a new excitement spreading over me, I stood ready for an adventure.

Not knowing what I was about to do, and how it would change things, but at that moment none of that was on my mind. All I knew was I didn't want to leave this man. He brought out this feeling in me I've never had before. Even though I don't know him, and he's telling me all sorts of strange things. This excitement just made me feel so alive, so free. At that moment my life changed without a second thought.

Chapter Thirteen

"**S**o, Rose, where would you like to go? Pick a place anywhere your heart desires. We can go to one of these places."

He points to the pictures that I was admiring before. I look again at the paintings. They each were of beautiful places.

My heart's desires where would that be? Where would I like to go? I've never gone anywhere exciting, or even been to the ocean. If there were no limitations in my way where would I choose to go? I pondered this for a moment. Hum, how about a mountain overlooking a beach? Something calming but exciting all in one. Though I don't know of a place off hand.

Oh how I wish I was more geographically accurate. All of the sudden a place popped into my head and I knew where I wanted to go. I could just picture it. Even though I didn't know how I just knew.

"Ogunquit Maine."

I stated. Where did that come from? I've never been to Maine. I've never looked anything up about that place. Let alone know that's where I want to go.

"Well then that's where we shall go!"

He clapped his hands together.

"Um, I know this is going to be a weird question but how the hell did I pick a place I've never heard of before and I'm sure that's exactly where I want to go?"

I asked dumbfounded.

He smiled down at me and asked.

"What did you wish for?"

He questioned me as he had this smirk across his face.

"Wish for? What do you mean?"

Oh wait my internal babbling I wished I was more geographically accurate. Oh my god I just wished for something and it came true? I wished that I knew where I would like to go and 'bam', it just popped into my head. This could get quite interesting.

"Do you remember wishing for anything?"

He prompted me after I didn't answer his question and continued to stare blankly into the abyss as I mind babbled to myself.

"I wished I knew where I wanted to go I guess in some way. I guess I got my wish!"

I shrugged my shoulders at him.

"Well, that's one way of figuring all this out isn't it?"

He smirked again at me but with a twinkle in his eyes that gave me a warm feeling spreading threw my body. Oh the things I would like to do with this man. I took a long deep breath in and said.

"Ok show me. How do we get to Ogunquit Maine?"

He grasped my hand a little tighter and gave me a quick squeeze with his hand and smiled reassuringly at me.

"So all you have to do is think of where you would like to go and..."

He took his free hand and as if he was sliding a curtain open movement type gesture he created a passageway. Like a doorway with nothing surrounding it. Just a shimmer of space splitting open before us. We took a step forward together, and all of the sudden there was a soft warm breeze with a salty taste. The air was fresh with a heavenly fragrance of wild flowers.

I look down at my feet and see that we are standing in a grassy meadow. The meadow is located on top of a large hill overlooking a rocky beach. The waves are soft and slowly crashing onto the small beach cluttered with rocks. I don't know how long I stood there just taking it all in.

"This is fantastic."

I murmured sounding all out of breath. I finally look up at him, and I realize that he's not looking at the gorgeous view before us. He's staring at me with the same look of amazement that I have but he's looking at me!

After a while of just standing there, staring at each other with warm looks passing between us. We finally picked a spot to just sit and talk. After a while I noticed I hadn't seen another person since the moment I came over to him in the park. I started looking around wondering where everyone could be. I know we are in a secluded area on top of this hill, but I can see the beach. And I don't see children playing, or fishermen in boats, no one.

"What's going on?"

I asked.

"What do you mean? Are you not having a good time? We could go someplace else if you'd like?"

He looked at me with a worried expression.

"NO, Christian, that's not what I was trying to say. I just got to thinking that I haven't seen anyone since we were in the park. Where is everyone?"

I asked as I motioned around with my hands.

"Oh, I see. Well I just thought that we could be alone. I didn't think you would mind."

He said.

At that moment something just felt wrong. I didn't know why, but I had the feeling that he was leaving something out. That there was a reason to why I haven't seen another living soul since we've started this life altering conversation.

Chapter Fourteen

I wasn't quite sure if I should be upset with him for hiding something from me, or be worried. I mean I know nothing about this man, do I? I started going over all the things we've been talking about. So, I know his name. His first name and nothing else about this guy. This good looking guy. Though looks can be deceiving. For all I know he could be a killer or a, oh I don't know a rapist. Ok I know that's going to the extreme, and he's given me no inclination that he's going to hurt me. Actually he's done the exact opposite he's shown me kindness, and concern for my well-being.

"So tell me something about yourself. I'd like to know more about you. I feel bad that I have only been asking you informational questions. Tell me something about you."

I said trying to gleam some private information about this stranger I've been spending the day with.

"Oh, ok I guess I could share something about myself but only if you are willing to do the same!"

He retorted with a playful grin.

"So how do you want to do this?"

He questioned me.

"How about we play twenty questions!"

I smiled shyly at him hopping he'd be ok with it.

"That sounds like a fun idea."

He beamed at me.

"So, I guess my first question would be what your last name is?"

I said.

"Oh, my full name is Christian Windfall. And what may I ask is your full name?"

He asked.

"Why my name is Rosalie White. And may I say that it is nice to formally meet you Mr. Christian Windfall."

I giggled at him.

"Why the pleasure is all mine Miss. White."

He did a graceful bow and took my hand in his. He gave me a gentle kiss on my hand. I blushed momentarily.

"So I guess it would be pointless to ask you your age as you already stated that you don't have one. So I guess my next question would be about your friends. What are their names?"

I asked curious.

"Well, I have a few close friends if that's what you're talking about. Their names are Sam, and Damien. How about yours?"

He countered.

''My two best friends are Emily, and Paige. How about what you like to do. Interests or hobbies?"

I looked to him hopping to push my plan into place.

"That's easy I love to paint. It's calming. How about you any hobbies?"

"Well, I like to work with clay, you know pottery, but I'm not good at it or anything like that."

Christian gave me this look, I can't quite figure out what he was thinking about so I just asked another question.

"What do you do as a pastime? Oh sorry that was a dumb question let me try that again. What are some things you enjoy doing when you're not painting?"

I asked.

"Oh, well you're probably going to get the wrong impression from this but I like to sneak peeks into your world. I enjoy watching the things your people create, and see how we differ. I know that sounds wrong to be watching people, but I've always been fascinated with your people. Does that sound bad?"

He asked me with a quizzical look.

"Well I guess that's no different than watching reality TV!"

I giggled

"I myself enjoy watching movies. So I guess that's not all that different."

I shrugged at him. Maybe we aren't that different I thought to myself.

"So where are Sam, and Damien? Could I meet them by chance?"

I asked with the hope to figure out why there was no one to be seen. This was it, if he made up some excuse to why I couldn't meet them I would know that he was hiding something.

"Oh, umm well they'er off doing what they do. You know messing around being goof balls and all that."

He stammered on and that's when I knew for sure he was trying to keep me away from people, but I wasn't entirely sure why just yet.

"So are you afraid they won't like me or I won't like them?"

I asked.

"Oh, no Rose, that's not it. They just are into extreme sports and stuff like that. They are always finding new things to try out, you know stuff like that. I would never be ashamed to introduce you to them. You are very interesting. I much enjoy being with you. You bring out feelings in me that..."

He cut off briefly.

"That are hard to put into words."

He finished.

Oh, wow. How can such simple

words make you feel so much? I smiled at him, but still I questioned him further.

"Than does it have to do with why you were so scared to tell me that you look into my realm or something? I just want to know why you're hiding me from others. Just tell me I really want to know the truth."

I gazed into his eyes, trying to convey to him through my thoughts how much I needed to know why he was hiding me.

"Yes, it has to do with me looking into your realm and the reason we are alone. I just ask that you don't get frightened, or upset."

He was looking at me like I was a frail little girl.

"Just tell me what's going on please Christian. I'm probably thinking it's worse than it really is. I won't get scared, whatever it is I think we can figure out a solution together. So what is it?"

I probed.

Chapter Fifteen

"My people have certain rules. Just as your people do. Some rules are stricter than others. One of our strictest rules is to stay away from those who believe in 'time'. Only the Council have the authority to view your realm. All others must have permission to do so. I shouldn't even be observing your people. I have not been given the Councils consent to be looking into your realm. If any of my people found out they would take you back, and we could never see each other again."

He sounded so sad when he said that, I just couldn't understand why.

"What, why? I don't understand why would it be such a big deal that you watch my people?"

This was not what I was expecting. I sat there just looking

at him. The anguish that was across his face was relevant. He looked. I don't know worried maybe. Worried about how I would take that information that he had just shared with me. Or maybe something else that he wasn't sharing with me.

"So why? Why is, it such a big deal that your people not look into my realm or watch it, or whatever they call it. What's the harm? If we shouldn't be able to see you as you have said then what's the big deal?"

I was starting to get frustrated. I know that I have just met this guy and we barely know each other, but the thought of not seeing him again frightens me. I don't think I could bare it. I shuddered at the brief thought. Why do his people think it wrong for us to be together?

"As I was telling you, we use to watch your people when they first created 'time'. We saw them changing. As the magic of 'time' got stronger it seemed to have taken on its own life force. 'Time' was in control of the magic of all those who believed in it."

He stopped to take a calming breath as if this was very upsetting for him.

"Our Council became concern for our wellbeing. Especially when one of the observers got pulled into the belief as well. They had just been observing when they were just pulled into the veil. Once they were inside the veil it was as if they just took on the concept of time themselves. Now they are trapped as well, with the rest of your people."

His eyes looked as if they had dimmed some during our conversation. He looked so sad. I didn't know why he had gotten so upset, but I could see the hurt deep in his eyes. His chest raised slower with each of his breaths, as though it was harder for him to speak. This subject must be very hard for him to talk about.

"What? That's crazy. How is that even possible?"

This information made me fearful.

"We aren't quite sure. That is why the counsel has forbidden others from going near the veil."

He said as he lowered his head.

"The veil? What's that?"

I asked extremely puzzled.

"I'm sorry, it's our terminology. But have you ever heard the saying 'looking through the veil of time?' Some of your people have used this phrase before. Your people, well how should I phrase it for you? Umm well I guess you could look at it as one of your hour glasses. The sand can move freely inside the glass but cannot escape the glass. We see the glass as a veil."

He stops momentarily to gauge my reaction, then he continues.

"For us it's a movable object, like a curtain. We can come in by sliding the veil to the side. As we once did. But after that incident our Council has forbidden us from going near the veil. They have become afraid that the magic of 'time' has grown so strong that we could become entrapped with no hope of escaping it."

Oh his eyes. At that moment they looked so sad, so lost.

"For your people it seems to be like the glass of your hour glass. An impenetrable force."

"Well, then how did I escape it then? If that is what they're so worried about wouldn't it be a good thing that I'm here? Couldn't they then see that there is hope of escaping it?"

I said hopeful.

"Yes, but I'm afraid that they might not see that as an exceptional sign that it's safe once more to view, or even cross the veil again. The creation has seemed to become an entity of its own, using your people as a form of energy to sustain it."

He said as he was shaking his head from side to side.

"Wow, that's kind of hard to think about. We think of ourselves as the highest on the food chain. To think that something is feeding off us is a little intimidating. But all those people."

I stopped for just a moment then went on with my thoughts aloud.

"It's not right to let them think there is an end. What happens if this cycle keeps going on and on? As you have said some or a lot of them don't even have souls. The ones that do keep recycling, splitting into pieces of themselves. What happens when they break their soul too many times? Is there a point in which the soul can't be fractured anymore? "

I didn't want to think about that possibility. It's just too hard to contemplate.

"That's just it Rosalie, we don't have the answers to those questions. We haven't been allowed to get close enough to see."

"Christian, I think it's important to try. We can't just let them be stuck like that. I think you should take me to your Council or something. They have to listen to us."

I tried to plead with him. It's just not right, we can't leave them to suffer in there.

"I know that we should it's just that I'm afraid of losing you."

He said as he took my hands into his own. We sat there looking into each other's eyes. It was as if he was trying to beg me or plead with me a silent message. I just don't know what to do. I don't want to leave him, but how can he expect to hide me?

Eventually someone will see me and question who I am, and where I came from. Not to mention how could I live with myself? Letting everyone that I know or even those who I don't know suffer like that?

Well I don't know how exactly it's really suffering, I mean was I suffering before? Well maybe I was. This is just too hard. I'm not sure, but I know that people have to be given a choice. So that was my decision. We needed to seek out his Council. That's when I decided we needed to try to help.

Chapter Sixteen

"Christian, I think I know where you are coming from. I too have strong feelings for you, but we can't be selfish. I wouldn't be able to live with myself knowing that there are others that I love, and care about stuck in an endless loop that one day could lead to the end of their existence completely."

I stared into his eyes willing him to understand from where I was coming.

"I understand Rose, I will take you to see the Council. But first I have to do this."

He put his right arm around my waist and pulled me into his embrace. His blue eyes never left mine until, with such passion he kissed me. At first, I was startled with the need, the passion that had overcome him. As it went on the kiss turned into a need. Like breath, I couldn't get my fill. I pulled myself closer to him. Our bodies moved in a perfect synchronization.

Soon we were two entities that had become one. Our tongues moved together stroking each other, taking what we so desperately needed from the other. In that moment life became clear I was made for this man. Our souls called for each other. My hands were tangled in his hair pulling him closer to me. It was as if I was trying to hold us together as one. His right hand slid up my back holding me close to his chest, as his left hand held my face to his. Gently he used his left thumb to caress my face.

We both were breathing heavily, as if we were running in a marathon at an astonishing pace. It was the best moment of my entire life. I felt exhilarated. Nothing I had experienced in the last eighteen years, could possibly compare to what his touch, his kiss made me feel. As we sat there all hands and lips passionately moving together I started to get the feeling that his need, his passion had an underlying meaning to it. It was as if he was trying to express a message to me.

Something that he was afraid to say. Or maybe it was that he couldn't find the words to speak.

If I wasn't so completely absorbed with the feel of his body against mine, or the touch of his ever so soft lips taking me on the ride of my life. I might have realized or heard what thoughts were rushing to my brain from the depths of my soul. In that moment there were no thoughts no realizations, or perceptions. My mind was closed to anything, and everything except this man. This glorious man that somehow in such a brief glimmer had stolen my heart, and every inch of my soul.

I never would have thought or even believed it possible to know someone, or feel about someone they way I did about Christian. Nothing, or anyone would ever be able to keep him away from me. I would go to the end of the earth to stay with this man. When all of a sudden, our passionate kiss was cut off by someone clearing their throat to get our attention. I swear I jumped ten feet into the air, and let out a girly scream.

Christian jumped as I did but he seemed to have a little more self-control. He managed to gracefully make it to a standing position, while placing himself firmly in front of me. As to shield me from the view of our unexpected intruder.

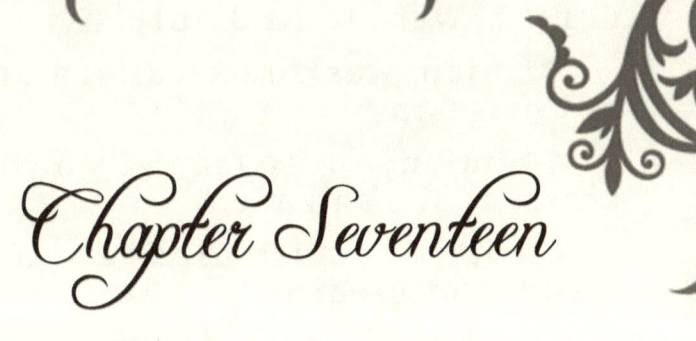

Chapter Seventeen

C hristian was standing in front of me with his arms in an outward position, as to block the trespasser from coming any closer to me. As I peeked over Christian's shoulders I saw the intruder who had interrupted the most magical moment that I had ever had.

He was tall maybe six foot, with blonde hair and green eyes. His body was that of a surfer, lean with tight muscles and a fabulous tan. As he looked at Christian, and myself he looked amused but with an underlying tone of concern. Christian was the first to speak.

"Damien, I know what this looks like but you have to understand..."

Damien cut him off.

"Christian please tell me you haven't crossed the veil? You know how dangerous it is. What if the

Council were to find out?"

Damien was practically glaring at Christian.

"Damien, I swear I haven't crossed, she saw me."

Christian murmured as if he was out of breath.

"Christian, that is impossible! Don't try to lie, we all know once the creation, 'time' has a hold of you it will never allow one to leave. So how could she see you? And who is she?"

Damien stopped and looked at me finally.

"Damien this is Rosalie White."

"Rosalie, this is my friend Damien Harper."

Christian used his hands to politely gesture Damien to myself and vice versa. At that moment my brain went completely blank. I'm not sure if it was because of how Damien was staring at me or what. I just stood there staring at him not knowing what I should do, or what I should say. A fear came over me, I'm not quite sure why, but for some reason I was afraid to speak. Afraid to tell him what I had just told Christian I wanted to do in front of the Council.

I looked back and forth from Christian, to Damien trying to figure out what I should say. What I should do when, Christian turned to me. In a soothing voice he told me, while slowly rubbing his hands up and down my arms as if to reassure me.

"It's alright Rose, I told you about Damien, he's one of my closest friends you can trust him, I do."

Finally my brain let my mouth have motor function again.

"Hi Damien, it's very nice to meet you! Christian has told me a lot about you."

I smiled shyly at him. Not knowing what he was going to do or how he was going to react to me I started to tell him.

"I was in I guess you would say my realm, just sitting there when I had a strange feeling and looked up. I saw Christian, and I guess I was just drawn to him. Unknowingly I passed through the veil as Christian calls it, and Christian and I have just been talking."

I flushed at the last part when it came to mind that when Damien came up to us we were doing way more than talking. Looking at Damien I could see him thinking, pondering the information that I had just given him to consider. When in a split second it was as if realization and hit him. He turned his look from me to Christian. All of a sudden it was as if it was just the two of them, and I was nowhere to be seen.

"Christian"

Damien exclaimed in a loud booming voice that took me by surprise.

"Is it... how can it be? Are you sure?"

Damien said.

I was lost. Is it what? Is he sure of what? I wanted to scream stop! What the hell are you to getting at when Christians response cut off my wayward thoughts.

"Yes, I'm not entirely sure how. But yes I'm absolutely positive. There isn't a doubt in my mind that it is."

He said with a huge smile plastered across his face. Ok this is getting ridiculous. Why are they being so collected, so encompassed? I was starting to think they were talking this way to

keep me from the conversation.
Why? what are they talking about?
Why are they leaving me out of it,
and acting like I'm not standing
right behind Christian. While the
two of them made me feel
rebuffed, or cast aside.

I was starting to feel like an
errant kid. A kid who had just
done something wrong, and the
adults are discussing the crime.
The crime in which you
committed. While awaiting said
punishment. The punishment
which is being figured out in front
of them. While the adults are fully
aware the child that they are
speaking of, is less than two feet
away, and can hear everything
that's being said about them.

Chapter Eighteen

*D*amien finally turned his attention back to me, with a look of astonishment, or disbelief. I couldn't tell which. When Christian took a step towards him and whispered something into his ear. Damien's look changed to perplexed, or confused maybe, I'm not entirely sure which.

Finally I spoke up.

"Could you two please include me in this conversation? I'm starting to feel excluded here."

Both of them turned to me with a look of dilemma spreading across their face. That's when I got worried.

"What?"

I snapped.

Both Christian, and Damien jumped from my outburst. Which kind of made me want to giggle.

But I held my ground and continued to give them both a chastised look. They looked between the two of them maybe trying to figure out who should do the talking. Apparently, Christian was the drawer of the preverbal short straw because he was the one who decided to answer my impending question.

"Well... Rosalie, what Damien was wondering was who you were."

He stated meekly.

"What do you mean who I am? I thought we were just introduced?"

I snapped back to him.

"Yes, he knows who you are now..."

He inferred with a sence of foreboding. That's when it hit me like a brick wall. They weren't talking about who I was now. All the conversations that Christian, and I had just had about the souls moving on into the lives of the children. The reincarnation. I hand never stopped to think that I was someone before.

After all that talk about people living, and dying I never stopped to think that I was a part of that never ending cycle. I have lived before. I've lived countless lives. I've been many, many different people who have lived. It all came crashing down as I tried to think of how many occasions in which I had died and been reborn? Who I must have been? All the lives I had lived before.

I just couldn't contemplate all that information. It just all became, too much for me to handle. Untill suddenly I no longer felt my feet touching the ground. The air swayed around me as I felt the blood leave my face, and I heard a deep ringing tone in my ears. There was pain pushing into my head.

The next thing I knew I was on the ground draped in Christian's arms. I heard him in deep conversation with someone. Oh it must be Damien. I had forgotten for a moment about him with all the thoughts running wild in my head. I opened my eyes after the ringing had dissipated.

"Oh, good she's coming too!" Christian breathed a sigh of relief.

"What happened to her? Is she all right?"

Damien asked Christian like I wasn't even there.

"I'm fine thank you, I was just a little over whelmed. But thank you for your concern!"

I said, probably a little snootier than I should have. But really I was tired of them talking about me like I wasn't even there.

Damien had this look all of a sudden, I'm not quite sure, but it seemed kind of like recognition. He took a sharp breath in and turned to Christian. His face paled and said.

"I think your right, it is."

"Ok, boys I've about had it with you two monopolizing this conversation. I want some answers and I want them now! While you're at it, cut the crap I know you two think I'm someone in particular. So spit it out already who do you two think I am?"

I practically shouted.

"Rose, it's just that you seem so much like..."

Christian started but cut off. It seemed that he was having trouble coming to terms with something. Not able to get past his momentary bewilderment. He just stood there looking at a loss of what to say, or maybe how to say it. Could I have once been something to this man? Could that be the reason I feel my soul is calling for me to be near him? As Christian and I just stood there staring deep into each other's eyes. From light brown to clear blue eyes. Our attention was brought back to the present again with Damien clearing his throat.

"How about I handle this Christian?"

He said.

"So Rosalie, the reason Christian and myself were discussing who you might be, or who you remind us of is because we, or should I say Christian lost someone to the creation of 'time'."

Damien was so sincere, it pulled at my heart.

Oh my god. So I could have been someone that he knew, or he knows, damn this is so confusing. How do you keep your alternate lives straight if you don't even remember what they were? Not to mention not even knowing that past lives could be a reality. Man I might just need a therapist. Hum, I wonder if they have therapists. I mentally giggled to myself. Wow this is some heavy stuff here.

To think we are doing this all in

the open on a hill overlooking the beach. I took that moment to look over the hill. As I did, I saw the ocean tide swaying back and forth. I saw seagulls as they flew low over the beach looking for food. Finally they both broke my concentration. They pulled me from my quiet reflections and asked.

"Are you all right?"

They both said in unison.

"Yeah, I'm fine. So who? Who do you think I am, or was, or whatever you want to call it?"

I asked as I shook my head, confused as all hell with the tenses, past or present.

Christian replied quietly with.

"I'm almost certain that you are Victoria."

It was almost a whisper. He looked almost in pain. I almost couldn't bear it to not rush over to him and hold him. To comfort him make him feel, I don't even know. All these emotions just came flooding to me in a rush. I'm not even sure from where they were coming from. I just knew I needed to hold him, to touch him. I just needed to be there for him.

Chapter Nineteen

My body went to him. Without any prodding from my brain. It was just pure nature. My soul finding its home at last. I didn't quite know how, but I knew at that moment they were right. I was her. Or she is me, man this is confusing. Do I have split personalities? Or are we, am I all the same?

Damien was the one who spoke next. "Rosalie, Christian, I'm sorry but we should really take this somewhere else. We wouldn't want anyone to stumble upon us. Not until we are certain of what we should do about this situation."

He looked from side to side as if he was expecting someone to appear at any moment.

"I don't know what to do. You can't hide me. I don't want to be hidden. I could never just stand by while there's a chance that others could break free too. It's just that I don't want to risk the Council forcing us apart. Could there be a safer way?"

I asked.

"Damien's right, we should go somewhere that's more secluded. Where did you have in mind my friend?"

Christian questioned Damien.

"Well, it should be someplace that no one would think of finding you. So I would have to say that place we would all go, do you know what I'm talking about?"

He asked Christian cryptically.

"Oh yes, I know where you're thinking of. I think we should travel separately. We should make some stops on the way so that we are not going there directly. Do you agree?"

His question was directed towards Damien. While I just stood there waiting, wondering when they would once again include me in the conversation. I looked back and forth between the two of them. Worry flashed across their faces.

"Damien, would you please take the long way around? We will be waiting for you."

"Yeah, sure my friend. I shall see you soon."

They clasped hands and pulled together in a quick embrace. Then Damien turned to me and ever so sweetly gathered me in a soft hug, and gave me a soft kiss on the cheek.

"I'm glad to see you again my friend. Please stay safe."

Damien said sweetly to me.

Then he turned and parted the air as I had seen Christian do. He took a step forward and he was gone. After a moment I turned back to face Christian. He still looked apprehensive, or anxious. He held his hand out to me and said. "Come we must go. I promise we will discuss this further, but for now I'd feel much better if we went somewhere that's more isolated.''

With that he held out his hand for me. I took it gratefully. Together hand in hand we stood. Christian parted the air with his free hand and together we stepped though the opening.

All of a sudden there was a room before us. In the room were shelves and shelves of books. The floors were made of a light wood, oak perhaps. There was a large window draped with a heavy, blue velvet curtain. Placed in front of the window, sitting across from the large fireplace, were two comfortable looking chairs. The ones you could curl up in with a good long book. The walls were covered in paintings. Looking closer at them I could tell they were like those that I had seen in Christian's living room.

"We're back at your place?"

I asked even though I was certain that's where we were.

"Yes but not for long. Let's get you something warmer to wear."

He left the room for a moment. While he was gone I decided to look at the beautiful paintings that hung on the walls.

Above the fire place hung a picture of a snow covered place. What made it catch my eye was the sky. The Aurora Borealis danced across the sky. It was spectacular. The colors just popped of the canvas.

As I stood there memorized by the way the colors swayed in the night's sky, Christian stepped up behind me. He placed his arms around my waist in a gentle embrace. He purred into my ear.

"That was always our favorite."

Chapter Twenty

I turned to him so that we were close, cuddling together. I looked up at him, seeing a hopeful gaze. I know what he wanted to hear. He wanted me to tell him I was or am, Victoria.

That I remember her, or remember being her. I just can't. I don't remember her or her life, or even if I was, or am her. How could I get his hopes up? Dose he only like me because he thinks I'm her? Dose that bother me? I just don't know. What if I'm not her? Would that change the way he feels about me?

He regards me reluctantly. As though he's trying to convey a question with his eyes. Finally he decides to speak his uncertainties.

"What is it my dear? What's got you looking so sad?"

As he was speaking, he took his

right hand to my face. Slowly he traced my bottom lip with his thumb. I didn't know what I should tell him. Should I tell him there's a chance that I might not be her? Should I ask him why he's so sure that I am her?

Leave it to me to fall for a guy that's not only from a different universe, but thinks in one of my past lives I might have been someone he knew. Someone he cared for. Now that I think of it I didn't even ask who Victoria was to him. Well I guess I just assumed because we were getting all hot and heavy that she wasn't like a cousin or a sisterly type.

Or whatever. I took a deep breath then said.

"You say ours like you two were a thing."

I sighed.

"Yes, we were 'a thing' as you say. I don't expect you to remember if that's what you were thinking. It's just that I've been sneaking to the veil sense I lost you... her it's confusing I know. I can't even begin to think how all this is for you but I can't help how I feel. My soul is drawn to yours. Can you feel it too?"

He implored, as he ran his fingers across my face. His eyes were wide, almost to the point of fear waiting for my response.

"Yes, Christian, I feel the pull your soul has on mine."

I responded as I looked deep into his clear blue eyes. He gasped and pulled me closer. Kissing the top of my head as he breathed deeply in the scent of my hair. I pulled back just far enough so I could look him in the eyes. I wanted to be able to see him as I spoke.

"So, because my soul feels a pull to yours, that is proof enough that I am or was Victoria? Is that enough for you? What if I'm not? Would that change anything between us?"

He cut of my endless questions.

"Rosalie, that is all the proof in the world. A soul can only be drawn to its other half. When you started to talk to me in the park I felt the spark, the gentle pull from your soul. I was afraid I was imagining it at first. I thought it was just my hope getting the better of me.

When we touched for the first time I felt the jolt, and I knew.

Please don't be mad at me for not telling you, I was frightened that I would scare you off. You already had too much on your plate. Not that it's any less full right now, but you said it yourself you feel your soul pulling towards mine."

His smile was infectious.

"Is it really that simple?"

I asked fearfully that somehow I might not live up to my former life, or whatever. That I might not fulfill his expectations from what he remembers Victoria to be, or have been. God this past tense shit is really getting on my nerves.

"Rose we will discuss this I promise but first we need to get you changed and get going. I don't want to rush you but I just don't want someone finding you before we have a plan."

He kissed me quickly on the lips and left the room to give me some privacy to change.

Chapter Twenty One

On the chair he had left me some pants and a sweater, along with a long beige jacket with fur trim along the hood and cuffs, and a pair of boots. I took off my flip flops and my shorts, and replaced them with the pants and boots. I pulled the beautiful cashmere sweater over my tank top. I took the jacket in my hand when there was a gentle knock at the door.

"It's all right you can come in, I'm decent.''

I replied. He slowly opened the door when I heard him gasp I looked up.

"What is it? What's wrong?"

I started looking around the room wondering what might have caused him to be startled. When I looked back he was standing right beside me.

"I didn't think seeing you in those close would bring back such fond memories."

He smiled at me. I never even thought to think where he had gotten them, or whose clothing he had given me. I guess I had just assumed he poofed them into existence.

"I'm sorry, does it hurt you to see me in them?"

I paused afraid to hear the answer. I don't know what she looked like or I looked like then. What if I'm not as beautiful as she was? What if he would prefer how she looked to how I look now?

"Don't Rose, I know what you're thinking. Don't do this to yourself. It's you that is here with me. You are the one that I desire. I'm sorry it's just that you triggered a memory of mine. Seeing you standing there in that outfit. Please trust that I want you. No one else. It's your soul that I'm drawn to not your appearance."

His words complete me. I don't know how this is going to play out, with my past life and his memories of another me. If that is what I am another me from another life. In that moment it didn't matter. Victoria or Rosalie, it wasn't the issue. All that mattered was I was his and he was mine. I rushed to him, as I reached his open embrace we heard a knock on the door.

Quickly he used his hand to part the air. Without saying a word he motioned for me to step through. I took the step forward, but when I looked back the door or whatever it is, had closed behind me. I had just stepped through the passage into what seemed to be the picture that had been hanging above the fire place. It was cold. Really, really cold. I put on the jacket that I still held in my hands and was glad I had time to replace my flip flops for the boots.

I took a quick look at my surroundings. All I could see was snow. Well that and the Aurora Borealis. They were fantastic, all the colors. It was as if they were alive dancing in the sky. Oh what I wouldn't give to just stay like this forever. When a thought occurred to me. No I don't want to stay like this forever. My forever wouldn't be complete without Christian here.

Suddenly I became frightened that I wouldn't see him again. I franticly started looking around. I had started to panic that he might have been taken. Or someone would follow him to me and force me back to the veil of 'time'. Who could have been at the door? What did they want? What was keeping him? Where was I, and how do I find him if I don't know how to travel? What was I going to do? Panicked I started looking around once again. Unexpectedly I saw a cabin in the not too far distance.

I started walking, the bitter cold bit at my nose. My eyes started to water from the sheer cold. The air smelled crisp, clean. Though it was refreshing it was extremely cold. I shivered. When suddenly I remembered something that Christian had said to me.

"All you have to do is wish it and so mote it be."

I had already had one wish come true, so what could I lose? I closed my eyes and wished to be at the cabin door. When I opened them I was standing right in front of the cabin door. Relief washed over me.

The cabin door opened before I had even placed my hand on the handle. I jumped back startled. When I looked up I saw Damien. He had a smile on his face and was just about to say something when a look of concern crossed his face. He looked from me to the beyond behind me.

"Where is Christian? What has happened why did he send you alone?"

The alarm was clear in his voice. He grabbed my arm and pulled me inside while checking to see if I had been followed. Apparently pleased that I hadn't been followed he turned back to me with an expectant look.

"So, what happened?"

He said with unease.

"We were on our way and there was a knock at the door. Christian opened the, oh I don't know what do you call them? Well he had me go though. I didn't realize that I had gone through without him till he had closed it behind me. I didn't know where I was, or where I needed to go. I had no clue how to get back to him. So I was looking around and I saw this cabin. It was too far to walk in the cold, so I wished I was at the door and when I opened my eyes here I was."

After my moment of babbling what had happened. I looked up to see the look of I'm not quite sure relief, mixed with amusement.

"What?"

I snapped. And that's when he started laughing and grabbed me into a big bear hug, and started to twirl me around in a big circle. Ok what has gotten into him? I'm here worried what has happened to Christian, and who was at the door, while he's twirling me around like a school kid laughing.

Chapter Twenty Two

He put me down, and took a pensive step back.

"I'm sorry, it's just you really are her. I was skeptical at first but, you are so like her."

He beamed.

"It's alright I understand. Could we please just focuses on what has happened to Christian? I'm starting to get worried."

I said as I looked around the cabin. There was a large wood fireplace, with a sofa and four chairs surrounding it. Behind the seating area was a table large enough to seat six people. The walls were a stained wood, with a few landscape paintings surrounding the room. I turned back to him and he motioned for me to join him over to the seating area. He sat on the blue sofa, while I chose to sit in one of the chairs across form him for a better conversational view point.

"Yes, we should figure out what has happened to Christian, and what we should do about you."

He remarked, calmly.

"Is there a way you could get a hold of him? Do you have a phone or something?"

I asked looking around for a phone.

"No nothing like that. We don't use those things. If we want to talk to someone we find them, or use our minds to reach out to them." He said like it was nothing.

"Wait, you're telling me you can talk to someone just using your mind?"

I gawked at him.

"I thought Christian was explaining all this to you? Or did you get caught up in other things?"

He smiled at me like he was trying to suppress a laugh.

"Give me a break, this is all new to me. He had said something about how when we took on the concept of time our brain stopped letting us use, or access all of our brain and that we only use a fraction of it. Is that what you mean?"

I inquired.

"Yeah, that would be the gist of it, I guess. So let me figure out who was at his place ok? Just give me a second ok."

He closed his eyes and took in a deep breath, then he exhaled. His face looked to be in deep thought. Then it appeared to be as if he was having a conversation. Though without moving his lips. It was his facial muscles that gave him away. He would scrunch his nose or turn his head. Little movements that you don't think about while you're in a conversation. You're too focused on what's being said to see how the body reacts to things you say, or do while talking. It was fascinating to watch.

He looked up and opened his eyes. My heart fell. I knew that something was wrong.

"What is it? Did you talk to him? What did he say?"

Panic stricken across my face.

"It was two members from the Council. They were there at

Christians place."

Damien informed me.

"What? Oh no, what does this mean do they know?"

"They are still with him. He couldn't give me much to go on without them being curious to who he was talking to."

His eyes looked as if they were trying to calm me.

"So what did he tell you?"

I asked getting a little impatient. This is just so frustrating. It's not enough that my entire world has been twisted and turned over and over again. Now this happens. I just hope they don't do anything to him. I wonder what they do for punishments for breaking the rules the Council has in place. I don't even know the extent of the rules.

"Well, for one thing he said not to panic. He doesn't think that they know about you. He wants us to start to think of what our best option would be. Also he wanted me to make sure I keep you safe till he can get to us. He wanted me to make sure you get something to eat."

"What? He wants me to eat!

Now... what is he thinking how could I possibly eat?"

"Rose, he wanted me to remind you that we are not in your world. Things are not as they seem. We don't have day or night. There is no concept of 'time' remember."

He lifted his right eyebrow at me in a half glare.

"Your body has become accustomed to a certain set of expectations, or a type of schedule. Christian is just worried that you will forget about your body's needs while you are too busy worrying about him. When did you eat last?"

He prompted me.

"Oh, well. It was before he and I traveled to Maine."

That got me wondering how long has it been since I came here. How long have I been gone? Wait I mustn't think like that. 'time' isn't real, it doesn't exist. It holds no meaning. I repeated this to myself till I had a firm grasp on myself. When I looked up Damien had a puzzled look on his face but didn't question me.

Chapter Twenty Three

"So what can I get for you? I assume he hasn't gotten around to showing you how this all works just yet has he?"

He said with a soft smile, not quite reaching his eyes.

"No he didn't get to that just yet. So are you going to show me then?"

"Sure, ok well he told you about wishing and all that fun stuff. I'm sure you saw him go through the motions right?"

He gave me a questionable look.

"Well I saw him swish his hands though the air. Is it like this?"

I asked as I move my hand as I had seen Christian do once before.

"Yeah you've got it. The reason we use our hands is so the magic knows where we want what we are creating to go. If we just wished say for an apple, and didn't hold out our hand there is a good possibility that the apple would appear above your head, and clonk your noggin."

He beamed at me with a small chuckle.

"So, is it necessary? No. But it can come in handy, or be a good idea. Especially if you want something large or heavy. So think carefully about what you want, then wish you had it while using your hands to direct the magic to where it needs to form, and..."

His hand swirled creating a mist, till he stopped palm side up. When the mist dissipated there in his hand rested an apple.

"Now your turn. Think about something you'd like to eat. How it tastes what it looks like, what it smells like. Now close your eyes. It will help you focus. Think about what it is. As you use your hands to show the magic where it needs to go, and it will materialize in front of you."

I had closed my eyes. Thinking about what I wanted. I could see it in my mind's eye. I could smell the juiciness. I could practically taste it. I used both of my hands to swirl what felt like soft silk around and around, till I felt a sense of completion. My hands stopped their undertaking. I held out my hands and envisioned where I wanted them.

There was suddenly a weight in my hands. I opened my eyes and saw what I had just used magic to create. I was thrilled. A girl could get use to this.

I smiled before taking a huge bite out of my double decker hamburger, smearing ketchup all over the corners of my mouth. I didn't care though. Damn, this burger tastes good. In my other hand I held my french fries.

Hey you can't eat a burger without french fries. If you can you're just not human. Well at least in my book any ways. Out of the corner of my eye I saw Damien smirking at me. I looked over to him and it looked as if it was taking all of his will power not to roll over laughing.

"What?"

I said around a full un lady like bite of my burger.

"I'm sorry it's just that you look like you've never eaten before. Just the way you're forcing it into your mouth, like its air you need to breath."

He started chuckling.

"Well, I'm so sorry if I'm not eating lady like enough for you sir."

I shoved the last of my wonderful hamburger into my mouth and as I was chewing I flicked my hand and made a napkin appear. Damien gave me an approving look.

"Well I guess you are a fast learner."

He mused, with an approving look plastered across his face.

"So, how about we get down to business. What do you think we should do about the Council?"

He said with a business like under tone. What did I want to do about the Council? Maybe I should find out what they might do to me first, or what they might do to Christian before I make any rash decisions.

Chapter Twenty Four

"I think that before I make any hasty decisions, I should know more about your people. I don't even know what your rules are or how you enforce them."

I looked at him in anticipation for his answer.

"Our rules, yes Rosalie that could help with your decision."

He nodded in agreement.

"Could you just try to explain them to me so I know what I will be heading into?"

I asked with a heavy heart.

"Yeah, sure. Well our most important rule is to stay away from the veil. We are not allowed to pass through it, or even view through it unless we are given specific permission to do so. Which doesn't happen very often if ever, I might add."

He paused to give me a side ways glance.

"Other than that we just follow simple rules such as not harming one another, not taking things from others. With the use of magic there isn't a need to take something from another. We can create anything from magic with just a thought."

As he was speaking he flicked his wrist and a swirl of black mist or as I was beginning to understand it; it was magic. When the haze cleared he held a sparkling jewel. Putting the beautiful jewel down beside him he said.

"See, there's no reason to take from another so the rule is kind of moot. Once the wise men created 'time' we have had some more rules added to what we had previously had. No one is to create anything in reference to the creation of 'time'. Nothing to hold or measure that creation."

He paused momentarily to take a breath.

"As your people invent things so to say, we are limited in that aspect. Your people have phones and cars and music players. Things that we hold no use for. Your people use those things to also hold your 'time' we can create anything as long as it doesn't hold 'time' with in them. Like this."

He waved his hand again. The magical mist appeared once again. Now there was a small device within his hand. It appeared to be an *I*-pod. I took the device and looked more closely at it. I touched the screen and it came to life. A music icon appeared. I tried to search for the music list but there was nothing else to it. I looked up at him with a puzzled look. He smiled at me and said.

"You need to use magic to make it work. You need to think what you want it to play."

He shrugged at me.

"Well what songs does it have on it?"

I asked dumbfounded.

"It can play whatever you want it to play just think of something. And..."

He closed his eyes and suddenly the device started to play a soft melody. Something like a lullaby. It flowed in a soft rhythmic tone.

"So it doesn't hold the music it

just plays it?"

I questioned.

"Yes I guess you could think of it like that. We are very careful with things that we imagine, we wouldn't want to give something too much power. Not like they did. Does that help any?"

He asked me.

"Yes I think I see where the Council is coming from. Trying to learn from the mistakes of those men. What they created took over and in a sense trapped them. They don't want anything to take over or gain too much power over anyone."

I stated.

"Essentially yes that is their thoughts."

He agreed.

"So what are your methods of punishment? What do you do if someone breaks the rules? Do you have jails? Well how would a jail cell hold someone if you can freely move from one place to another with just a thought and a swish of your hands? Or the fact that they can create something with magic to break free of your entrapment?"

I asked Damien.

"Yeah, that was one of the Councils problems that is why they created the Enther."

He replied.

"Enther. What is that?"

I said with a puzzled tone.

"Well it's hard to explain exactly what it is, but it looks like a bracelet that they clasp around your wrists. When you are wearing it all magic is, I guess you could say rerouted to the wearer of the other set."

He pauses I think to make sure I'm still with him.

"So the person who is serving punishment, doesn't control their creations entirely. They are I guess you could say pre-approved by the Council. So they are unable to travel or make anything that could allow them to break free from their as you called it cell? They can still make food and clothing, but certain things are kept from them. Such as travel."

He shrugged at me.

"So if the Council found out that Christian has been breaking the rules by viewing through the veil, they would lock him up. Using the Enther to stop him from leaving. Is that all they would do to him? When would they let him go? How do they decide when he should be released?"

I questioned.

"Well that's where it's impossible to say. For you, you see 'time'. You count down. We don't see life that way. For you to understand you would have to know where they are taking him."

He stopped as if to gauge my reaction.

"We don't have a building per say that houses criminals such as your people do. I know if I tell you, you are going to freak out, and go into a panic. So before I tell you, you must keep an open mind. We can create anything out of nothing. We don't house the limitations as your people see them. Anything is a possibility. Your people have taken on beliefs that hold no purpose. Are you ready?"

He asked me with a timid glance.

Chapter Twenty Five

"Yes, I am willing to keep my mind open to all possibilities. Now can you please tell me?"

I said with a bit of frustration radiating off of me.

"Our criminals as you would like to call them, well they are sent to a different place. Not a jail or cell but to a different planet."

Damien looked at me waiting for my response, like I was going to totally freak out by what he had just said.

I think my eyes popped out as my mouth hit the floor.

"What?"

It was barely a whisper.

"I knew you would freak out."

He said exasperated. As he rolled his eyes and scooted closer to the end of the sofa, so that he was closer to me. He reached out his hands and placed his right hand on my leg. In a reassuring pat, he tried to pull me out of my frozen like state. What in the world? I mean how is that even possible? Yes I understand they can travel where they want with practically the flick of their wrists.

Really I am just at a loss. How can they breathe? Do we just believe that there isn't oxygen in space or something? I took a couple quick breaths and went back to reality.

"Ok, please explain. I'm listening."

I sat there looking at him waiting for him to explain how it was possible for them to go to other planets, and all that craziness. When I guess I came to an understanding with myself. If magic was real how could anything else not be plausible?

"Wow, you are taking this way better than I expected."

He said looking completely shocked. I guess because I didn't scream and pass out or something completely damsel in distress like.

Well I guess I'm just going to have to take this new world as it is and understand that the life that I knew was a lie.

"Thanks. I guess, can you please just tell me how it works. I promise that I'm ready to keep an open mind and not let my pre conceived notions to hold me back. Christian's life is in our hands along with all those souls who are still trapped within the veil of 'time'. So can we get this over with so I know what I am stepping into? Please."

Wow I'm really getting to a calm circumstance.

"I'm sorry. Your right we should get through this. Ok, your people have come to certain beliefs, and those beliefs are controlled by the "concept of time". The more you believe that something is a certain way, The magic controlled by the collective of 'time' makes it so."

He shrugged.

"Your people believe that life isn't sustainable on other planets, and that we cannot live there. They can't see what is right in front of them. We can go or do whatever our hearts desire."

Damien told me matter of fact.

"This is really kind of cool. So are you saying if my heart desired to go to the moon?"

I asked with a hopeful tone.

"Yes, you can go anywhere your mind can imagine."

He said with a light blazing in his eyes. As he looked at me I felt a new sense of excitement. Oh how I have always dreamed of going into space.

"Really!"

I exclaimed in a breathy whisper. He nodded to me.

"Anything is possible. So does that help you? Do you know what you want to do about the Council?"

He asked me with a hopeful look in his eyes. What do I want to do? How do I decide what the right thing is? I don't want the Council to force me to go back, but I can't leave all those people to be trapped.

Leaving others to suffer only to protect myself would be selfish. I would never be able to live with that decision. How am I going to go about this with the Council? How can I convince them that there is a chance for all those who are trapped to be saved?

I don't even know how I was saved from the ensnarement of 'time'. What can I say to them that will convince them not to send me back? Or not to send Christian away? This might just prove to be harder than I thought.

How are we going to come up with a plan if I don't even understand how I came to be here? Oh what are we going to do? I just want Christian back. To feel if arms around me once again.

"What is keeping Christian?"

I asked Damien. I was starting to become fearful that he had been sent away for looking for me.

"He is fine I can assure you that nothing has happened to him. He will come to us when he feels that it is safe for him to follow." Damien remarked.

"He said whatever you decided he would be ok with. So the decision is yours to make."

He exclaimed.

"Well, then I think we should go to the Council. We should tell them what happened with me, and try to come up with a solution to help others, if the Council will allow us."

I looked to him so see what he thought about my plan.

"Do you know what you want to say to them?"

Damien asked with a look of apprehension.

"Well not exactly, what do you suggest?"

I just don't know any more. Why does this have to be so complicated?

"We will figure this out. I promise. So you want to go to them and tell them how you saw Christian through the veil and managed to cross back over. Is that correct?"

"Yes."

I responded.

"Well I don't see any other way of explaining how you crossed without implicating Christian, are you willing to do that? Even if it means that they might send him away and you back, all for the chance that you could help others find their way out?"

He asked me again.

Is it crazy? Should I be willing to be sent away, with the chance that I won't be able to break free once again?

"Yes, that is what I'm saying. I think that's exactly how Christian would feel too."

I looked up at him and saw him nodding his head in agreement, with a hint of a smile to his lips.

"Certainly, I agree that is how he would feel too. Are you ready?"

He said as he stood and held out a hand for me. This was it. I might be going back, or sending Christian away. This is the right thing, right? I'm not making the wrong decision am I? I need to stop questioning myself. I need to step up and do the right thing. It's not all about me and how I feel. There are so many people who don't have a choice. I stood up, taking a deep breath I took his hand. I turned to look Damien in the eyes. I nodded to him and said.

"Let's get this done. Do you want to go with me or do you just want to open the... hey what do you call it? I forgot to ask you."

I looked to him and awaited his answer.

"We call it the Aperture. Furthermore I wouldn't allow you to go without me."

He opened the Aperture, and we stepped through.

Chapter Twenty Six

After we passed through the Aperture, we were standing in a building. It reminded me of a court house. The walls were a polished stone. There were benches lining the hall. In front of us was a large wooden double door.

"Wait here, I'll be right back."

He said. Then he closed his eyes, like he did when he was talking to Christin before telepathically. He nodded and proceeded though the door. Moments later he returned and together we went inside. We were standing in a large room. At the front of the room it looked like where a judge would sit, but instead of one judge's seat there were five.

In front of us sat three women and two men. It was a strange sight as the authority figures who you would assume to be elderly, looked the same as Christian and Damien. Knowing that time doesn't exist, I still have a hard time with everyone looking the same age concept.

The man on my far left was handsome with black hair, and brown eyes. He was eyeing me with a look of skepticism. The woman who sat aside him was blonde, wearing a grey pantsuit. She had a questioning glair. Next to her was another blonde woman, this one was wearing a navy blue dress. I couldn't tell what she was thinking, she gave nothing away.

Next to her sat the other man, you could see he was very muscular even though he was completely covered with a dapper suit. Lastly, was the third woman. She was giving me a hopeful look. This made me feel slightly better. She was beautiful, with long wavy brown hair that flowed down past her bare shoulder. She was wearing a green ensemble with a side strap covering only her left shoulder.

Damien steps forward to address them. "Council members, I would like to introduce Miss. Rosalie White."

He stepped aside and motioned

to me using his left hand.

She has escaped from the grasp of the creation that's is called 'time'."

Suddenly the room that had been silent enough to hear a pin drop, erupted into a roar of gasps.

Two of the Council members stood and took a defensive step back. As if I could make them disappear just by standing too close to them. Ok this wasn't quite the reaction I was hoping for. Before they could decide to force me from the room or whatever I found my voice.

"Please, I'm just here for your help."

I said in a hopeful tone. I was gazing at them with soft eyes and a timid smile.

"Our help?"

Snapped the man whom had stood, and leaped away retorted with an angry voice.

"Sit down Markus."

Commanded the woman who I was unable to read her facial expressions. She took command of the room. Standing she smoothed her navy blue dress. She took her gaze from the man she called

Markus, and turned to face me.

"Please excuse his ill-mannered outburst. Continue with your testimony."

She gestured with her right hand for me to continue as she ever so elegantly sat back in her seat.

"I would like your assistance, helping others escaping the clasp of 'time' as I did. I think it is a possibility, and we are duty bound to help them. We can't just sit by and let them continue on until there is nothing left of their souls. It's inhumane!"

I was almost to the brink of shouting. I need to control my volume I reminded myself.

"Pray tell, what would you have us do?"

The muscular man inquired. With a quizzical look.

"Yes, timeling. What would you want us to do? They are the ones who did this to themselves."

Pantsuits interjected. I stood there for just a moment before I spoke up. The women at the center of the table turned to pantsuit and said.

"Sasha. Please keep your cross

words to yourself."

Her face still didn't give much away, but she kind of had an undertone of annoyance. Then she turned to muscle man.

"Clay, don't be so cynical. We have kept our distance because we were fearful that once the creation known as 'time' had a hold of you it was impossible to escape. This girl..."

She turned to me and continued.

"Is our proof that escape is a possibility."

Her face softened as she looked at me before she continued.

"We as leaders of our people owe it to them to seek options out if there truly is hope for these lost souls. Do you agree Evangeline?"

She turned to the beautiful woman with the beautiful curly brown locks. I turned my gaze towards Evangeline.

"Helena, I agree with you. The timelings are also our people. We owe it to them to consider any ray of hope that could be a plausible attempt to end their suffering within the veil."

Evangeline seemed determined

to make her view on the subject clear. Markus, Sasha, Helena, Clay, and Evangeline all turned their gaze back to me. The discussion was now on. The fate of my old world now rested on my shoulders. No pressure.

Chapter Twenty Seven

Markus and Sasha apparently a couple, were strongly against any attempt trying to save those who were ensnared in 'times' grasp. They believed we would be risking the creation known as 'time' coming for us all.

Dooming everyone to suffer the same fate as the timelings, as they've come to call us. Clay seems to be bored not caring as long as he himself isn't put in harm's way. Helena the leader of the Council and Evangeline are the only two who seem even a little concerned for the well-being of the souls trapped behind the veil. Sasha, and Evangeline, continually quarrel back and forth, with the pros and cons to helping them. The attention is promptly brought back to me when Clay interrupts the woman's disagreement to question me.

"So Rosalie, how did you manage to break free?"

Crap. I was hoping to avoid this question.

"I was drawn to my soulmate."

Please don't ask me any more please. I don't want him to be punished for looking for me.

"Who dear, is your soulmate?"

Helena asked. Crap!

"Christian. Christian Windfall is my soulmate."

I said as I felt a rush of guilt spread over me for giving him up so easily, but I had to. He would understand, well at least I hope he would.

"I see my dear, could you explain to us how you found him? I ask only to come to a conclusion to how you came to find yourself on the other side of the veil. Please this could be the key to saving others like yourself."

She had such a kind reassuring face. I truly thought I could trust her. So I went on.

"He was looking through the veil close to where I had been sitting. My soul was drawn to him. I guess I followed the pull of my soul to the other side of the veil."

I had my head down, and was fiddling with my fingers, while I confessed to the crime I now knew Christian had committed. I looked up from my knotted fingers to see the look of shock on four of the five faces in front of me. Clay, Markus, and Sasha were gapping at me. While Evangeline just looked shocked.

"Helena, he has broken our most important rule."

Markus snapped appalled by my testimony. Helena closed her eyes, and just as I had seen Damien do she appeared to be talking to someone. She nodded then opened her eyes once again.

The next thing I knew Christian was standing aside me. I couldn't keep myself from launching into his arms. He too, seemed pleased to see me once again. For a moment it was as if we were the only two in the room.

My hands were tangled behind his neck. His arms embraced around my lower back. I pulled just far enough away to give him the briefest kiss. Taking my hand, Christian, and myself turned and together we faced our judgment.

Helena looked down on both of us. I couldn't tell what she was thinking. She has one good poker face. I glanced from side to side, trying to get a feel for their position, were Christian and I stood. Finally Helena spoke. She looked directly at Christian.

"Christian Windfall, you have been accused of breaking our strictest rule. Please inform us, what do you plead?"

Helena boomed in an authoritative voice.

I glance from Christian back to Helena. My mouth was popped open. No, they can't be mad at him! He saved me from the clutches of 'time'. He risked his life for mine not even being sure he would ever find me. This is wrong. What are they going to do? Please don't punish him I thought to myself.

"I plead guilty of the charges, Council members."

He bowed his head and held his stance as if he was awaiting their ruling.

"So say the Council, what is his punishment for his crimes?"

Helena boomed with such a loud

voice for such a small person. I looked from member to member, as if trying to silently convey my plea with my eyes.

Each member closed their eyes. Each of them appeared to be having a heated discussion. This was actually quite interesting to watch. They need not speak out loud, nor did they have to leave the room for privacy. They could talk freely to each other in their minds.

Chapter Twenty Eight

A thought popped in my mind of how much of the mind I still didn't know how to fully use yet. Man I must seem like a chimp to them! That's kind of an unpleasant thought. I must try and figure all this out.

Wondering how I could learn all what the power of my brain could accomplish. I just hope I would have Christian as a teacher. I didn't know what I would do without him. I looked over to him. He didn't look up at me, but he gave my hand a quick squeeze.

Suddenly I heard him speaking to me. I was looking right at him, but his lips were not moving. Holy shit he was speaking directly into my mind! It is one thing to know that it is possible to speak from the mind, but to actually hear someone's thoughts was fricken awesome. A smile spread across my face as I listen to what he was telling me telepathically.

"Rose, I know why you had to tell the Council of my viewing through the veil. Please do not think that I am mad in any way. I love you! I always have and I always will. If I had a chance to do it again I would. Even if I had never found you I would never have stopped trying to find you. Trying to free you from your imprisonment."

He took a moment before he continued as if he was taking a deep breath.

"I would do anything for you. You are my love, my life, my reason for being. You are the air for my lungs. Without you I could not survive. No matter the consequences, I am willing to pay the punishment for my crime."

He gently caressed my hand with his thumb. I realized that I had tears streaming down my face. I wanted to talk to him, tell him that even though I have only know him a short while, I too felt the same as him.

Oh how I wish I knew how to tell him what I need to say, as he has just done for me. I wish I could tell him that *"I love him."*

All of the sudden he gripped my hand a little tighter. I looked over to him. He didn't look up, but I saw his smile stretching across his face.

"You figured that out faster than I had expected."

He said.

What? I thought to myself confused by what he had just said to me within my mind.

"I can hear you!"

He replied to the question that I had flowing around in my head.

"What? You can hear me I'm talking to you telepathically?"

I asked him apparently with my thoughts.

"Yes Rose, you are. You never seem to stop amazing me. I love you, please know that. I'm not afraid of the punishment as long as I know you are safe, and I will find my way back to you. Do you understand?"

Christian asked me.

"Yes, but I just found you. I don't want you to leave me. I'm not ready for that."

I practically begged him. Our telepathic conversation was abruptly cut off with Helena's voice filling the room once again.

"The Council has come to a decision. For your crime you must serve the punishment of banishment. This is the law as it has been written since the discovery that the creation known as 'time' has the ability to pull viewers within its grasp."

She paused momentarily.

"You shall serve your sentence of banishment to the planet of the Councils choosing. It has been agreed on that the place you shall serve as your sentence is one of Saturn moons. Titan shall be your prison for one obit around the sun. There you shall be left alone in solitude, to think about the crime in which you committed."

Helena commanded the room in her loud authoritative voice.

The next thing I knew there was a loud gasp. I looked around to see from whom the noise had come, when I realized it was my own. I clasped my hand to my mouth. Tears were on the brink of pouring down my face. Helena spoke calmly to me.

"Rosalie my dear, this is our way. I know your people also have punishments for committing a crime. We do not die as your people believe. He will not be harmed. He will return to you just as he is now."

Her eyes were gentle, like she was talking to a fearful child.

"Do not fear for him, we only want him to learn that the rules that we have put in place are there for a reason. They are there to protect. We do not harm our people that would be inhumane. Please do not think of us as cruel."

She said.

"I understand, but what does that mean for me? What are you going to do with me?"

I asked. I was slightly afraid to hear what they were going to rule as my verdict. The Council members all looked at Helena. Helena placed her gaze upon me.

Chapter Twenty Nine

"Well Rosalie, this is the subject where the Council members are torn. Half would have you return to your people in fear that the creation 'time' will do anything to obtain you once again. The subject of rescue for the other timelings would be to leave them as they are. Trapped, doomed to serve as sentencing for the crime of fabricating a dangerous creation."

She stopped only momentarily to look from one side of the Council members, to the other side of Council members. Facing Christian and myself again she continued.

"The other half of the Council would like to pursue a rescue attempt of the timelings. For you serve as a form of proof. Proof that to escape from the creation of 'time' is a plausible feet. The decision is left for me to decide."

She took a moment, and looked around the room.

"I can see where both sides are coming from. I must think of everyone. For this decision could turn events for both sides of the veil. Depending on the outcome."

Again she paused. This pause seemed as if she was considering what she was going to say.

"It could turn out to be damnation for those of us on this side of the veil, if I come to the wrong decision. Do you understand where I am coming from? I must think of how this could affect the lives of so many people."

Again she paused as if she were weighing all of the options that lay before her as carefully as she could. I understood her position. If the creation known as 'time' did have the capability to come after me, it could expand. Ensnaring those previously untouched by the creation called 'time'. Also giving it more magic to power itself. It would be unfair of me to risk their lives by staying. Nonetheless, they are just sitting by allowing others to suffer. They are afraid to try and help those who are trapped.

Helena started to speak once more stopping my train of thought in its tracks.

"I am choosing to incorporate the will from both sides of the Council member's views into my ruling."

She said matter of fact. Christian gasped beside me.

"No, please I implore you. Please no!"

It was almost to the point of a whisper. She momentarily shifted her gaze to him before returning to me.

"The Council's verdict is that we will execute a rescue attempt of the timelings, but you will be the one to attempt this feet. Both sides of the Council get what they want. One side gets you back to the other side of the veil."

She turns to face Markus, and Sasha. They both smile a nauseating smile. Then she turns to Clay, and Evangeline and says.

"In addition we get the chance to save some souls from their entrapment."

Helena stated.

I looked to Clay, and Evangeline. My eyes caught

Evangeline's briefly. She gave me a reassuring smile, and nodded to me. Helena continued, and I turned my attention back to her.

"As the head of the Council I decree that whomever you help free from the entrapment of 'time' will be given asylum. This will include yourself if you are once again able to emerge from the veil. However, you shall only be allowed to cross once. If you find yourself back on this side of the veil we will not allow you to cross again. Do you understand?"

She stopped, and awaited my answer.

"So you are saying that you are exiling me back to my people, so I can try to save them. Only I have to do so without moving freely from realm to realm. It would be a one way trip? Am I correct?"

I questioned her.

"Yes, you must find a way to help others break free without crossing yourself. Once you cross that would be the end of the rescue mission. You would be leaving the rest of the timelings trapped within the veil."

Helena replied.

Chapter Thirty

S uddenly I was reminded that Damien was in the room, when he spoke up.

"Pardon my intrusion Council, what if Rosalie is unable to free any souls? What if she is unable to free herself again from the veil? Will you leave her trapped?"

His voice sounded slightly worried.

"Damien, we cannot risk more people being lost within the creation called 'time.' She wants us to help them. Therefore she must be the one to risk being trapped once again. She is the only one to have been on both sides and remember that there are two realms."

Helena took a moment to glance in my direction.

"Who is to say that if we send someone over that they would be able to remember why they are there? She knows both realms. Again the Council has come to its judgment. The sentencing will commence."

Helena spoke in a loud booming voice, and clasped her hands together.

"Please, I beg of you... please just allow Rosalie and myself a moment alone to say our goodbyes. For the chance we might not get to see one another again. You may restrain me with the Enther, so that I am unable to escape if that would make you more comfortable."

Christian pleaded with the Council.

"As you wish so mote it be. I will open the Aperture to a holding room for your parting. I trust you Christian, the Enther will not be necessary. You must be prepared when I reopen the Aperture to the holding room. Do you understand?"

She asked us both. We both nodded in understanding.

"Yes, we are ready. Thank you Helena."

I said. I turned to Christian just

as Helena opened the Aperture.

Together we stepped through. Once on the other side, Christians seized me into his strong arms. Our lips found each other. We were all hands and lips moving in perfect synchronization as if they had never been apart.

I explored his body with my hands. My mouth never leaving his. It was as if we didn't need air. All we needed at that moment was each other. How could I live without this man?

The thought of never seeing, or touching him again. Never kissing his strong but soft lips. The thought threatened to tear me apart. I couldn't think about this not now, not knowing that Helena would be back to take both of us away from each other. Each of us off to our own imprisonment.

For in this moment all there is, is him and me. He, is my everything. Christian halted our passionate kisses for just a moment. Just long enough to magically craft an extravagant king size bed in the middle of the empty room. I hadn't even noticed the surroundings which I had stepped into. I hadn't cared. All that mattered to me was holding on to him for as long as was given to me.

In that brief moment, when he had created a magnificent king size bed that was covered in plush pillows, and wrapped with luxurious satin sheets, I got a sense of the room we were in. The walls were a soft baby blue. There were no windows or doors. It was like a box. Within the room there were only a couple of chairs scattered in various locations. The walls had a few paintings scattered around.

Once the bed was fashioned that's when my world really changed. He looked onto my eyes. He placed his hands on my face, holding it in place. It was as if his eyes were drinking me in.

"I vow to come back to you. If you are not on this side of the veil by the end of my sentencing I will cross the veil. I'd rather be trapped in the creation that is 'time' than live without you. Do you understand? I would rather die a thousand deaths than to continue on without you."

He said in an out of breath voice from our passionate kissing.

"Then I will have to vow to be

here before your sentence is through."

I closed the distance between us, and pushed him down on the bed. As I was kissing him once more I wished there was nothing between us. Suddenly, I felt as though I was being wrapped in the softest silk. We were being picked up from off the bed. When we were upon the bed again both of our clothing was gone. Christian chuckled at me as he said.

"Rosalie, you sure have a way of doing things. Are you sure you don't remember more than you've let on?"

He wiggled an eyebrow at me.

"Shut the hell up and make love to me. I need this to last me till we are reunited again."

I used my right hand to pull his face back to mine as he started to make sweet love to me.

Chapter Thirty One

Without the concept of 'time' sex becomes a whole new ballpark. There was just him and me. The give and take from our bodies. The sensations were that of nothing that I had ever felt before. Reaching higher and higher with each other, again and again. Only stopping when we both were completely spent.

As we lay there our bodies completely intertwined I looked over to him. I took my hand and started to trace the outline of his face. He looked at me and said.

"God how I have missed you."

His eyes sparkled as he gazed upon me.

"If only I could remember."

I gazed into his eyes.

"Will I be able to communicate with you during your

imprisonment? I'm new to all this you know."

I said.

"Well you know how to telepathically speak now. We should be able to speak, but... I'm not sure if it will be possible from within the veil. When you were pulled into the veil I tried, and tried to reach your mind. It was if you had disappeared."

His eyes dimmed as he revealed this information. What? When I was pulled in? Was I the viewer they were talking about? Is that how I became entrapped with in the veil? If that's what happened how was I supposed to help others escape? Little own escape myself?

"Are you saying that I was the one you told me of that was viewing the 'timelings' when the creation of 'time' ensnared them?"

I asked in disbelief. My heart was pounding fast with the anticipation of his answer.

He took a deep breath and nodded his head as he continued.

"Yes, you were the viewer who was yanked into the veil. I wanted to go after you, but the Council forbade anyone from going near the veil without prior permission. I had to find ways to sneak to the veil. I've been looking ever since."

He had such passion as he said this.

"I will do it again if I have to. Remember that. Just hold on to the truth. Don't let it take over you again. If you practice your magic, and don't use any inventions that hold the creation that is 'time', maybe that will be enough to keep it at bay. Just try to telepathically communicate with me. I will always be listening."

He took me in a strong embrace.

"I promise I will do my best. I'm so sorry that I got sucked onto the veil. I will try my hardest to make it up to you. For all that you have had to go through."

"You know when you asked me why, or how I could have that look of disgust on my face when looking at that old couple?"

He asked me simply.

"Yes. That's the reason I'm here right now. You never did tell me why you had that reaction to them."

I looked up at him from within our embrace.

"I never told you the reason I was giving the old couple that look... well, I would have to say it was a mix between loathing, and sorrow. They found love. It was the one thing in our realms that never changed."

His voice was soft but it was filled with so much emotion.

"So why were you looking at them that way?"

I was curious, and confused.

"Because, they would be torn away from each other, all because they believed it had to come to an end. If they were lucky enough to find each other again and again they would still be doomed to keep the cycle of losing each other with the chance that they might not find one another ever again. All because they believe in death. There is no reason for their souls to ever be apart, but the creation 'time' is going to doom them to spend eternity loosing each other over and over even if they find each other. It just hurt me to watch two souls be separated from their other half's. All for nothing. It all could have been prevented if the creation 'time' had never took control of them."

I now understood. He didn't hate them. He was disgusted by their circumstance. He was watching what he viewed to be what had happened to us all over again. I held on to his strong arms. We stayed like that just taking in all that we could till the Aperture opened once again. We both got up and closing our eyes while we used our magic to once again clothe ourselves. Just before we stepped through the Aperture Christian grabbed my forearm, stopping me from passing through. He held out his hand.

Within his opened hand his magic swirled. When the magic rescinded there rested a silver locket. Christian took the locket and placed it around my neck. Once he had it secured around my neck he opened the stunning locket.

It had a charming design carved into it. Within the locked inhabited a picture of Christian on the left. The picture on the right was of him, and myself. We were in an embrace while we gazed into each other's eyes. It was as if someone had snapped a photo of us while we were lying in bed together. Well with clothing on.

"To help you remember. And so that we are never apart again."

He took the locket and tucked it under my sweater that I had dressed myself in.

"Thank you I will never take it off. I love you."

I told him as I gazed into his love filled eyes.

"As I you Rosalie."

We kissed once more before stepping back through the Aperture.

Chapter Thirty Two

Helena was standing on the other side when we emerge from the Aperture. For once I could see emotion plastered across her face. She had a look of foreboding. I knew this decision was a hard one for her to make.

She had to be the leader. She had to show a firm hand, and still try to rescue those who had been confined in the creation of 'time'. I was willing to take this endeavor, even though there was a chance I might not be able to find my way back through the veil. It was a risk that I was willing to take. This was something I believed to be a noble cause. One that Christian had done for me.

Risking my life for the chance that others could too be saved. The risk was worth it even if I could only save one soul. Though I hoped to save many more than that.

Thinking to myself I started to ponder how I was going to pull this off. If Christian hadn't been in the park. If he hadn't been viewing through the veil, I probably wouldn't be here. I wouldn't have ever been able to escape. I wouldn't be having these mental ramblings.

I was drawn to the thought of what would have happened. What would have happened if I hadn't stopped my unpacking to try and clear my thoughts. Giving myself a chance to ponder what decisions I needed answers to. What would have happened to me if I had just stayed in the apartment? Stayed to watch movies with Emily and Paige, and procrastinate about my over bearing life decisions? I was brought back from my endless retrieve when Christian gave my hand a light squeeze. I turned to him and he pulled me into a strong embrace. My soul felt as though this was our last chance. I held on to him as if my life depended on it. Too soon I had to release him. He gave me one last kiss goodbye before Helena spoke to us.

"What way would be easier for the two of you? Who would prefer to go first?"

Helena said in a remorseful voice.

"Send Christian first."

I jumped in quickly.

"I don't want him to have to see me cross the veil again. He has already had to endure that pain when I was seized by 'time'. Also maybe seeing him sent away from me will help my soul remember what I am fighting for."

I said as I looked at Helena.

Christian nodded in agreement with my decision. Christian held out his hands as Helena placed the Enther around his wrists. They looked like silver band bracelets. She cuffed them around his wrists. While she herself wore a similar one around her right wrist. Hers had small blue jewels incased around it. Then she waved her hand to open the Aperture.

"Your sentencing will be complete with one cycle around the sun. Think of how you came to be in this predicament. Marry meet and Mary part, and marry meet again."

She bowed her head in a slight goodbye. Christian took one last look over his shoulder and said.

"I love you my dear, safe travels. Please come back to me. Remember what I told you. Follow your soul back to me. I will see you when I return from my punishment."

He gave me a look that held such deep meaning in it. Then he turned once again, and he was gone. It felt as if my soul had just been kicked in the gut. All the air had left my lungs, unable to fill with new air. I had this pain in my soul that throbbed. All I wanted to do was curl into a ball and cry. I didn't know how I was going to function with this devastating pain that was rocketing through my mind, body, and soul. Helena placed her hand on my back in a gesture of support before she spoke up.

"Now it's your turn, my dear."

She turned to face me.

"For you the trip will be a little different. Come I will escort you to the veil. Do you have a preference to where you cross?"

I hadn't thought of that before. I wiped my hands across my face, and took a painful breath in. The air felt like knives. It scraped and cut its way down my throat all the way to my lungs. From there the knives stabbed my chest as the air was accepted into my lungs. My lungs were happy for the relief of air, but cringed at the pain from the lack of air I had, had. I pushed past the pain to ask Helena my questions.

"So you can't just open the Aperture into the veil?"

I questioned her puzzled by this information.

"No, we don't dare attempt to try. We wouldn't want to have an open pathway leading to that creation. If the creation that is 'time' got ahold of the Aperture, it could hold grave consequences. Who's to say that wouldn't give 'time' free rain over both realms?"

She lifted one of her perfect eyebrows at me and then continued.

"When you were pulled within the veil we discovered that those on the other side could not see us. It is quite fitting that you are the one to attempt this rescue."

She smiled kindly at me.

"How did you know exactly, that we couldn't see you?"

I questioned.

"We knew when you were looking right at him and it was as if he weren't there at all. He was yelling to you pleading for you to cross back over. I was the one who had to order the guard to restrain him from the veil. It broke my heart to see how he was suffering but I couldn't risk others trying to save their loved ones."

She stopped momentarily to take a deep breath. She let it out slowly just before saying...

"I had assumed that he had been sneaking to view the veil, but I could not prove it. I hadn't wanted to try and prove it ether. I have regretted keeping him from you since it happened. I didn't see the need to punish him, but when you told the Council of his crime I had no choice but to uphold our law. Please don't hate me for the judgment I had to pass."

She looked saddened by the realization she had just shared with me. I could see that she too had suffered a loss, and for that I couldn't be angry with her.

Chapter Thirty Three

"I am willing to forgive you. All I ask is that you share some information with me before I cross the veil. I need to know as much as I can so I can find a way to save the others."

I hoped she didn't think I was trying to stall or anything. I just felt that knowledge would be an important key to saving as many souls as I could.

"Yes that would be a smart approach. I agree with you there. Thank you for your forgiveness, I feel terrible for having to pull you two apart. Especially after you two have been apart for so long. I know this will be hard for you both to be apart. But for the chance that we might be able to save those we have feared to be lost to us forever it is a worthy cause. Well, at least that was what I told myself when I passed your judgment. Thank you

Rosalie for coming forward."

She enveloped me in a gentle hug. Straightening up she smoothed her beautiful green dress. When she looked at me again her face was back to her "normal" I guess... poker face.

"Come we shall go to my chambers to deliberate the information that might come in handy for you and the other timings to escape from the sands of 'time'."

As she said that it made me realize so many of your saying referencing 'time' could be omens. Maybe we have been trying all along to escape 'times' clutches. The things we say. Stop watches for example, yes they probably got their name because the can calculate your measurement of 'time'. But what if subconsciously our minds were trying to warn us about the creation of watches. Also why did we call them watches? It made me think about everything we said about the creation. Why did we call the front of a clock a face? The parts that move around, we call hands. We had been trapped by the hands of 'time'. A shiver ran through my body as my focus went back to my surroundings.

Helena closed her eyes and began having a telepathic conversation with someone. I wondered to myself who she was talking to. When she looked up, and waved her hand for the Aperture to open. Together we stepped through. She walked with purposeful stride towards a large chase lounge. Helena motioned for me to sit where ever I pleased. I took a quick look around the room.

It was a large white room with elegant furnishings. Among the chaise lounge there were several reading chairs, and a large sofa. Each adorned with decorative pillows in blues and browns.

The walls may have been white but the room was filled with such vibrant colors. The walls were filled with paintings and lush curtains that hung over the windows. Looking out the window I saw rolling hills, with green grass covering the field below. The sun was shining and birds were singing.

The floors were hard wood with a large area carpet in the middle of the room. I felt relaxed in her chambers. I picked a reading chair that was across from the chase which she had chosen to sit. I turned my attention back to her as she asked.

"What information do you seek before your journey? I shall try to help in any way that I can. So please don't be afraid to ask me whatever it is that you feel you need to know."

Helena looked relaxed and ready to answer any questions I might have.

"Christian explained to me how the creation that is 'time' was created. I think I need to know a little more about how things work on this side of the veil. Christian explained that when we took on the concept of 'time' we lost the ability to use all of our minds. I also think it could be fundamentally helpful if I understood the veil itself. I have picked up a few things like telepathic conversation, and wishing, but I need to know how to gain access to the deepest parts of my mind."

I stopped to take a breath, and think what else Christian had told me.

"Christian explained that our fractured minds may be keeping us from using or remembering the magic that we hold within. So could you help me to gain access to the other portion of my mind?"

I questioned. She took a deep breath before she answered my question.

"Rosalie I can only try to help you on that endeavor. I have never had to teach one how to use something that we were created with. I shall try my best to be your teacher. As to helping you with remembering I don't know how I could help with that. Maybe if we work on regaining the use of your magic you will be able to find the answers that you are looking for."

She looked confidently at me. I just hope I can figure this all out, as the fate of the world is literally resting on my shoulders! No biggie I thought, as I mentally rolled my eyes at myself. Ok I need to stop babbling and get down to business.

"So where should we start?"

I asked kind of puzzled how can you ask someone to teach you something you don't know, when you don't know what it is that you don't know? This might just be impossible, but we have to try.

Chapter Thirty Four

"You said you picked up telepathy, that's a good start. Have you learned how to use magic yet?"

She eagerly asked me.

"I have wished for things and gotten them, and Damien showed me how to..."

I closed my eyes and pulled the magic from within me to swirl in my hand. I concentrated on what I wanted to fashion. When the magical mist dissipated there in my hand laid a ball of light. I moved my fingers in a dancing motion, and the light danced along with them. Helena nodded in approval. I closed my hand and the dancing ball of light disappeared.

"That is very good. Telepathy, wishing, and the control of your magic, this is good. Have you learned how to move objects with your mind?"

Helena asked me, like what she had just said was no big deal.

"Telekinesis?"

I barely whispered. This is going to be awesome I thought to myself.

"So I take it that is something that you have not learned yet?"

She gave me an assured smile. She looked to the sofa and with a wave of her hand, one of the turquoise pillows flew across the room, and landing in her hand. A huge smile spread across my face. Yep this is most definitely going to be fun.

"Now all you need to do is, focus on the item that you want to move and envision where you want it to go. Think of it like you are nudging an item. Here let's use an object for practice."

She closed her eyes and with magic created a figure. When her magic dissipated I could see it was a wooden object similar to a chess piece in size.

"Here we will use this for practice. Imagine in your mind that it's being pushed by an invisible force."

She instructed. I looked at the figure, I started to think how it would look if it was sliding across the table. Suddenly it slid a few inches across the glass table. I beamed with excitement.

"It's kind of like using a muscle."

Well one that doesn't move or that is actually there. Ok maybe that wasn't the best analogy. Maybe like using an invisible hand? I don't care, this is Fricken awesome!

"Yes it is sort of like using a muscle."

She smiled back at me. Even though she probably was thinking how stupid that sounded.

"I think you got the idea of telekinesis, it really isn't hard. I don't see you having a problem with continuing on your own. With practice you should be fine. Rosalie, has anyone taught you how to selfheal?"

She asked me with one of her eyebrows tilted up in her question.

"No, no one has told me that was a possibility yet so... no."

Wow we really have forgotten a lot. All because of the creation of 'time'. I thought to myself.

"Well then, it really is simple. Your body my dear knows when it needs to heal, it does it on its own. Your people have just forgotten how it should work. It really is all about visualizing. You just need to focus on the injury and think of what needs to be done to correct the situation. Say that you cut your hand. You would think about the skin and how it needs to mend."

She instructed me though my training.

"Wait it's that simple? You just think close and it mends it?"

How did we forget all this? I thought to myself.

"Well, yes essentially you think close, but you need to focus on the act your body does to close a wound. Your body sends blood to the spot and clots to help close the gap. Then the skin regrows. Now, if it is a deep cut, you would need to assess your injures first. Making sure that you haven't nicked any arteries. Or anything like that."

She shrugged at me.

"Your mind controls everything.

If you'd like to think of it as watching it on your creations, the ones you call TVs. Close your eyes. Think about a part in your body. Focus on what its function is. How it works. You can see it in your mind's eye. All you need to do is think it and your body will respond."

She looks at me waiting. What do I say? Life is getting really interesting.

"Ok, I think I understand. I can repair any injury, all I have to do is first asses the extent of the injury, then think how it needs to mend or whatever and my body will take care of the rest."

As I was talking I was twirling my fingers in my long brown hair.

"Let's try something fun!"

She said with a huge smile on her face.

"What do you have in mind?"

I asked with a butterfly flapping around in my stomach. What was she going to do slice my hand with a knife or something?

"What do you want to do?"

I asked sheepishly. Oh please don't do anything gross. I have a weak stomach I don't think I could handle her slicing my hand open just for the fun of learning how to piece it back together. The though gave me creepy chills.

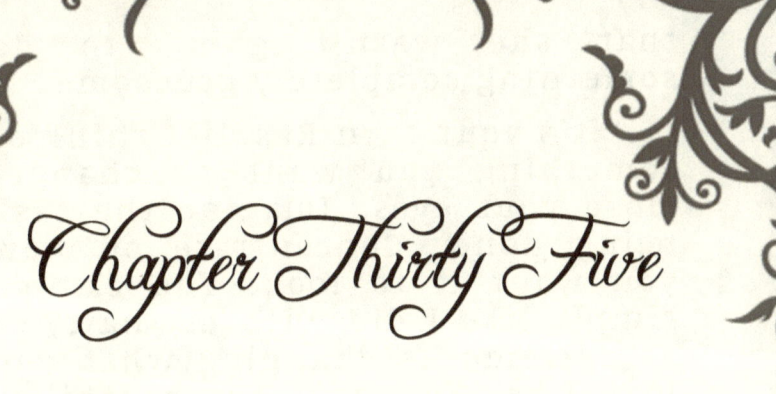

Chapter Thirty Five

"Rosalie, don't look so worried."

She started chuckling.

"I know we were just talking about healing, but we can learn how to manipulate the body in other ways. I wouldn't inflict pain just to show you how to heal."

She lifted her right eyebrow at me and smirked.

"Oh come on Rosalie don't be frightened. Here let me show you. It's all about concentrating on what you want the body to do and..."

She took her hands and placed them at the top of her head where her hair line began and pulled her hands over her hair. Suddenly her hair went from blonde to brunette.

"I so did not see that coming."

I laughed with a sigh of relief

that she wasn't going to do something completely gruesome.

"It's your turn Rosalie, think of something you want to change, close your eyes. Imagine the task being done. Concentrate on how you want it to look. You can go simple like I did with my hair, or as extreme as changing what you look like. You have the capability to change anything on your body as you see fit."

She opened her eyes so that they were wide with mischief clearly gleaming inside them.

"It's limitless. If you would like to be taller just tell your body to grow a couple of inches. Our bodies do as we bid of them. I know in your realm you believe yourselves to lack control. There is so much your people have backwards. The things you have come up with. All the sickness and sadness, it all comes from the feeling of having no control. They believe that they are sick, and bam the creation of cancer."

She said with an annoyed tone in her voice.

All that suffering for what? I needed to get them out of there. We have it in our capability to fix anything from a broken nose, to ending cancer. To think all the suffering we have been going through. With all the science we have we couldn't even touch the surface of what we have locked away in our minds. I need to practice, I need to learn how to help others so I could help them help themselves.

"Hum... What should I do?"

I pondered out loud as I looked to Helena for some ideas then it came to me. I closed my eyes and thought of what I needed to focus on. I put my hands over my face and took a deep breath. I concentrated on what I wanted to change. I told my body what I wanted it to do. When I was sure I was done with my task I pulled my hands away from my face. I looked up at Helena. I saw a smile flash across her face, as she nodded with her approval.

"Very good. I love your new nose, and you changed your eyes from brown to blue. Where did you get inspiration from?"

She asked me curiously.

"I have always wanted to have blue eyes and I hate those color contacts, but this is so much cooler than wearing contacts! Oh and I've always hated my nose, but I would never be one to go get surgery done to fix something."

I told her as I shrugged my shoulders.

"What else can we do that I don't know about yet?"

I asked her with eager curiosity.

"What about flying? Have you attempted it yet?"

She said in the calmest voice ever. Damn her awesome poker face.

Meanwhile my mouth popped open again, and hit the floor. So she's telling me that I can defy the laws of gravity? I think I might be in heaven. Ok I really need to focus. I need to learn as much as I could, so I could pass through the veil and start trying to help others cross. I closed my opened mouth and as calmly as I could manage said.

"No Helena, I have not attempted to fly yet."

I managed to say with a straight face, even though I was bouncing like a giddy two year old when their parents say they can eat all the candy they want. This was going to be a lesson that I would never forget. Man how great could this get? First I found my soulmate, who told me that 'time' doesn't exist. And so as long I didn't believe in the creation called 'time' I would never age or even die.

Then he showed me that magic is real and even I could wield it. I had been shown all these awesome things that I didn't know the mind was even capable of. Such as telepathy, and telekinesis. Learning how I was capable of repairing any injury. Even being able to manipulate my body how I saw fit. Now I found out I could fly. Really this was so fricken cool.

Chapter Thirty Six

"Well then Rosalie..."

She stood from the lounge, and looked at me with excitement in her eyes. She held out her hand and said.

"Are you coming Rose?"

I looked back at her with eager anticipation. I stood as I took her hand.

"I am so ready for this. Let's go."

Helena smiled at me and opened the Aperture. Together we stepped through. On the other side I saw we were standing in a large open field. It was surrounded by rolling hills. I wondered where we were. The field was covered in purple wild flowers.

The smell was so crisp and clean. The sun was shining bright. The sky was bright blue with scarce clouds scattered about. There was a gentle breeze, swaying the beautiful flowers. It was as if they were dancing. I was so excited I was all but jumping up and down.

"How do I do it? Do I just have to think happy thoughts?"

I smirked to myself. Helena gave me a puzzled look.

"I think you might be laughing at me. I'm not entirely sure why, but no. You don't just have to think happy thoughts to fly."

She raised one of her perfect eyebrows at me as I was giggling like a school girl the Aperture opened and Evangeline stepped through. I didn't know if I was going to be in trouble or what was going to happen. Evangeline turned to me and greeted me with a warm smile.

"How are the lessons going?" She asked Helena.

"Well if you ask me I think she is a very quick study. Yet again she has done all of this before in, what do they call them past lives? Yes I believe that is what they are called."

She turned back to me.

"Rosalie, you should really try and remember who you once were. It might be helpful for you. Though for now I am willing to help you understand all that you forgot. Are you ready for your flying lessons?"

She looked at us wiggling her eyebrows at Evangeline, and myself.

"Helena, I think she should probably learn to hover before she learns to fly."

Evangeline suggested.

"Well, if you think that would be a good idea I am willing to take the advice. She leaned over and gave Evangeline a small kiss on the cheek.

"How about you take this one?"

Helena said as she sat down on the ground in a relaxed position. Evangeline turned to me and started explaining what hovering detailed.

"So Rosalie, I want you to close your eyes and clear your mind. Let go of all your insecurities. All of your fears. Take a deep breath. As you exhale I want you to envision all of those emotions and fears leaving your body."

She took a deep cleansing breath and released it slowly. I followed along by closing my eyes as she had instructed. I cleared my mind and took cleansing breaths as she had said.

"Feel how light it makes you feel. Hold on to that feeling of weightlessness, use it to lift you up. Don't let that feeling go. Take deep cleansing breaths. In and out, in and out. Now Rosalie, I want you to open your eyes."

Evangeline said in a soft voice.

I had felt all of the stress that I had been holding on to. It just left my body with my exhale. It was as if a large bolder had been sitting on my shoulders. As I released them the bolder had rolled off of me. It was freeing. I took another deep cleansing breath. The sun felt brighter, the wind felt as if it was caressing my face. When Evangeline told me to open my eyes I felt one with my body. I had never felt this way. So connected, so free. When I finally got around to opening my eyes I went to look at where she had been standing beside me. But she wasn't there.

I looked around with a fright. When suddenly I hit the ground. You know when you have a dream that you're falling and you actually feel yourself hit the bed. That's exactly what happened to me. But I had actually been in the air. I looked around and saw Evangeline, and Helena snickering at me.

"Was I just hovering?"

I said with a bit of excitement.

"Yes that's why I wanted you to open your eyes, but I guess I should have given you some warning to stay relaxed! Well lesson learned, are you ready to try that again?"

She smirked at me again.

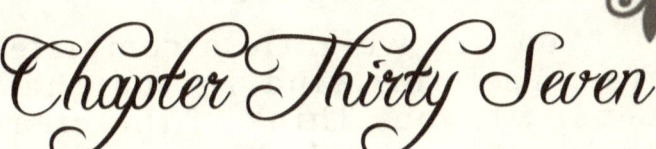

Chapter Thirty Seven

"*Y*eah! That was totally awesome."

I said.

"So eager!"

Helena laughed at me from her flowery seat.

"Hey, I don't know about you but that was one of the coolest experiences of my life. So please excuse my eagerness to learn more."

I retorted a little sourly. Helena nodded at me with a look of understanding. I felt bad for snapping but turned back to Evangeline for her help.

"Please help me again Evangeline. I'll be ready this time.

"Ok Rosalie, now I need you to calm down. Feel your heart beat slowing down. With each breath you take the lighter you are.

Breathe in the air and release all
of your baggage that tethers you to
the ground."

She took a deep breath.

"You are weightless completely
free. Feel the wind in your hair.
Let it fill you. Think of the breeze
as it blows, let it be your guide.
Follow the sway of the breeze and
relax with the sway of the air. Now
slowly open your eyes. As you do
try your best not to get too
excited. Remember to breathe in
the air and release all that holds
you on the ground."

She coached me again. I took a
couple of deep cleansing breaths. I
did as Evangeline said. I
envisioned the air filling my body.
I released all the stress and
worries that the world held within
me go out with each breath. Again
I felt the air around me lifting me
up. I let the breeze calm me, and
be my guide.

This time I tried my best not to
get over excited as I slowly opened
my eyes. Staying as calm as I could
I looked around. I was only
hovering about a foot or two off
the ground. Oh how exciting it
was to have the weight of the
world no longer pushing me down.
The absolutely freeing feel to have

the air completely surrounding me. I looked around. Everything seemed different from just a few feet above the grounds surface. I could see all of the field we were in. All the flowers seemed to be swaying in the breeze as if they were putting on a ballet just for me. I turned my attention back to Evangeline, and Helena.

"So how do I move around? Do I pump my arms like I'm swimming in the water or something?"

They both looked at me like they were trying their very best not to burst out laughing.

"No, there is no need to swim."

As Evangeline said that Helena erupted into a burst of laughter. As she fell backwards she started to roll around on the ground.

"Hey..."

I snapped.

"I'm new to this be nice."

I said grumpily.

"I... I'm sorry I just imagined you as a fish swimming in the sky. I just couldn't help it please forgive me."

Helena said through bouts of laughter.

"So what do I do then?"

I asked. While I closed my eyes again and tried my best to stay calm and keep breathing steadily. In with the air and out with the weight of the world. I repeated this over and over till I calmed myself down again. When I felt calm again I reopened my eyes. When I looked around again I was even higher in the air, maybe three or four feet in the air. It was exhilarating.

I had a new insight into the world, which I just know realized I know nothing about. I turned my attention back to Evangeline, and Helena. They were smiling at me like mothers. Mothers who were proud of their young child who finally got something. Something that after trying for so long to get, they finally got it right at last. They made me feel accomplished.

"Oh Rosalie, you're getting it!"

Evangeline said proudly.

"Now if you want to move around imagine the wind is thrusting you. Pushing you in the direction that you desire to go."

She continued.

"Oh, ok I think I can manage

that Evangeline."

I said as I thought of wind propelling me in the direction that I wished to travel. All of a sudden the wind picked up and I started to gently glide across the sky. I reached my hands out to feel the wind flow through my fingers. It was so exhilarating. Every inch of my body was surrounded by a gentle caress of the soft wind. I let out a giggling shrill.

"This is so amazing."

I turned my body so that it circled around. Flying back to Helena, and Evangeline.

"Now Rosalie, to land back on your feet just slow yourself down. To a pace you can walk to. Then slowly let yourself down. Just before touching the ground start walking and you should land gracefully."

Evangeline made it sound so simple. Well how hard could it be? I did one more lap around them. Enjoying every dip and sway in the open air. As I approached them I thought about the wind slowing down to barley a gust.

Turning my body so that I was in a standing position. I slowly lowered myself so that I was just above the ground. Just as I was about to touch the ground, I guess I got over confident and the wind picked up. Pushing me faster than I could keep up with. As my feet touched the ground, I was shoved face first into the field.

Chapter Thirty Eight

"Ok, it's harder than it sounds."

I said as I spit dirt from my mouth. I slowly pushed myself from the ground. I felt a stinging pain in my hands. Looking down I saw my hands were both covered in small brush burns and shallow cuts. Great, this is just wonderful.

"Are you alright Rose?"

Helena and Evangeline said together. You could see that they were trying to control their amusement.

"Yeah I'll be fine. I just need to practice that landing I guess. Could one of you get me a cloth to wrap my hands with? As I assume you don't have a band aid?"

I said as I was looking at the extent of my injuries. They both gave me a strange look. "What?"

I asked.

"Have you forgotten something?"

Helena asked me as she raised an eyebrow at me.

"Oh, yeah I can heal myself. It's been in my nature to bandage my injuries."

I said as I shrugged my shoulders.

"You must try and remember all that we are teaching you. The last thing we want is for you to be trapped once again by the clutches of 'time'. If you don't hold on to these lessons there will be nothing we can do for you. Now let us look at what you are going to need to do, to correct what you have done to your body."

Helena took my injured hands in hers.

"Oh that's nothing at all. You should have no problem fixing that."

As Helena said that Evangeline peeked over her shoulders to see what I had to correct.

"Yeah Rose that will be a simple fix. Have you and Helena already gone over healing?"

She looked at me, waiting for my response.

"Well, we discussed it but I haven't tried it yet."

I said.

"Well now here is your chance. Try closing your eyes. You seem to focus better that way."

She insisted. So with her instruction I closed my eyes.

"Now, think about what you need to do. First think about what hurts. As you are focusing on that pull the injury to the front of your mind. Do you see it?"

She asked me. Concentrating, I pulled the thoughts to my mind of what hurt. With my mind's eye, I saw my injured hands. I used that concentration to see how deep the cuts were. They were small, tiny cuts. I thought of how the body naturally heals our wounds. I used my blood to push away the bits of dirt that lay in the cuts. I thought about my blood clotting and my skin filling in the gaps. The throbbing that was in my hands slowly resided, until I no longer felt any pain.

When I opened my eyes I looked at my opened palms. My hands

were back to normal again. I gasped with joy. Helena, and Evangeline clapped their hands together celebrating my achievement.

"Fantastic, Rosalie."

They both mused.

"Now I think we have covered everything."

Helena said.

"You should be all set to go back through the veil, are you ready?"

She questioned me.

"That's it?"

I was momentarily set back. With the thought that I was being sent back threw the veil. The possibility that I might be trapped there unable to escape suddenly became terrifying. I must have zoned out as the next thing I knew Evangeline developed me in a warm hug.

"It's all right, you'll be ok."

She spoke softly to me as she gently rubbed my back in a circular motion.

"I don't know if I'm ready yet."

I said the fear evident in my voice. What was I going to do to convince others that 'time' isn't real?

"You'll do just fine my dear, you have picked all of this up very easily. It is as if some part of you remembers and is helping you bring it to the surface of your mind."

Helena said reassuringly to me.

"You just need to work on your memories. There isn't any way for us to teach you how to regain that which you have lost from your reincarnations. We are not even sure if you will be able to unlock those memories, as you are no longer within the body you were formed in. Who knows if your soul will be able to regain that which was taken from you?"

Helena said with a sad smile.

Chapter Thirty Nine

"Where would you like to enter the veil?"

Helena asked me.

"I guess the park, where Christian and I crossed would be best. So you can take me to Oak Hill Park in Eureka, South Dakota."

I said.

"I think you need to be the one to open the Aperture. It is the last thing you haven't done on your own."

She said to me.

"Think of where you would want to go. Focus on what you need to do. Use your hands to part the air."

"Like this?"

I questioned her as I positioned my hands like I had seen

Christian, Damien, and Helena do before. I closed my eyes to focus. I envisioned the Aperture as a doorway opening in the air. When I opened my eyes the Aperture was in front of me.

"I did it!"

I beamed. Together the three of us stepped through to the park. It was just as I had left it when Christian and I had been talking.

"I knew you could do it. Just as I have a feeling that you will be able to accomplish a great feat that no one has ever even thought possible. You have greatness in you."

Helena then gave me a welcoming hug. As I stood there, knowing that it wasn't my realm I looked around. I could see a shroud in the distance. It looked like a film that covered as far as you could see. The park was as I had left it, benches along the path with the fountain in the center. There was no one around. It was completely silent except the sounds of nature. Birds chirping in the trees. The sound of the water flowing from the fountain. There was a gentle breeze blowing through the trees. Though there wasn't a single person within the park. I thought this to be strange but shrugged it off.

It looked just like my side. As I thought that, I pondered to myself was it truly my side? It had been all that I had known up till just recently, but was it truly my home? No. It wasn't my home, or my realm. It was my prison. I must not think of it as home. My home is Christian. Where ever he was, that was where I belonged.

While he was serving his sentencing. I would be serving mine. I had to think of that place as a prison. I had tell myself over and over that no matter how much it looked and felt like home. It was my prison, and my key to getting out would be releasing the trapped souls within it. I could do this I told myself. I just need to keep it together.

"So how do I cross the veil? Do I just walk through it?"

I asked my acquaintances.

"Well, the reason we call it a veil as it's like a cover. Well, at least on our side. Your side seems to be more like your invention, the 'hour glass' I think that is what they call it."

She turned to me, and I nodded

in reassurance that she was correct.

"It holds the sand within. In their case they themselves are the sand. Trapped to continually fall through the top till you hit the bottom. The top as you would think of it as being life and the bottom representing death. Then they start all over again. A never ending cycle."

She said as she shook her head from side to side before continuing on.

"Before you were pulled in, our people would cross and explore their world. To see all of what they had done with their new way for living with their new creation. It used to be quite interesting to watch from within. Though we didn't approve of the concept we hadn't thought it to be harmful to us. We moved freely within their realm. Watching the others as they went on with their lives. We hadn't thought it harmful until they started their beliefs in their deaths."

She paused momentarily as she closed her eyes, as if this was hard to talk about.

"We tried to stop them from

this belief, but it was as if they couldn't see us. They would look right through us, as if we weren't even there. After the incident with you we stopped going through the veil. We gave up hope that there was a way for us to help them. I created a mirror which I could view the other side of the veil. I wanted to keep an eye on things as to make sure the creation was kept at bay on their side of the veil. I could see without being near it, to make sure the veil didn't expand. It was my attempt to keep the rest of our people safe from the clutches of the creation 'time'."

She said with a saddened voice. Evangeline put her arm around Helena, as if Helena were cold and was in need of some warmth.

"So, there is something that just doesn't make sense to me. The veil how large is it? I mean we don't have a cutoff point in the world. We haven't fallen off the end of the world so to speak. How does it well work I guess is what I'm asking."

I said kind of foolishly.

"Your people see the world differently as we do. You think of it as a 'time in space. Space moves freely here. You look at the world like an immovable object. Look at it, truly look. The veil is covering what the world truly is."

She paused to look around.

"Yes the world is vast, but as you have just done we moved through space to get here. When they created 'time' they made a rip in our space. They created, I guess you could call it a reflection."

Helena looked back at me with a shy smile across her face.

"It is as if there are now two worlds. Two of everything, everyplace. Didn't you see how our side wasn't cluttered with buildings? We live with nature. We don't destroy it. We only create when we need, not because we want to. When we are not within our structures we use our magic to put them away in sorts. They are not a permanent structure. We call them forth when we have use of them. They are not in one permanent location. We have the power to create as we see fit. Why would we want to destroy this perfect world?"

She said to me. That's when I thought about what she was saying.

Chapter Forty

While I had been here, I hadn't seen the outside of a building. Only the cabin, but it was as if it had just suddenly appeared out of thin air. Well with the use of magic you could pop a building in and out of existence whenever you wanted. So the veil was like an entrance to another universe?

"So you are saying that there are essentially two earths?"

I questioned afraid they would laugh at my question.

"Well I guess you could see it like that. When they created 'time' it didn't start off that way. Only once they created the inventions to hold their 'time' that was when the veil was created. That's when we believe 'time' started using the magic of those it trapped within."

Helena stopped to take a deep

breath in, then continued.

"It became like a mirrored version of the world. A separate realm. We could see it and cross over but once they believed in the creation they never crossed the threshold back to the real world. The world in which we were formed."

Helena explained to me.

"This is good. I need all the information I can get on the veil. So it is a completely separate world? Are there only certain points of entrance?"

I asked puzzled.

"There are many places you can cross the veil. How about this..."

She waved her hands in a circular motion and stopped with her palm facing up. Magic swirled like a foggy mist till it dissipated, leaving a clear sphere.

"This is how you see the world correct?" She asked me.

"Are you going to tell me the earth isn't round?"

I gawked at her with my eyes popped out of my head.

"No, I am just making sure that is how your people see it."

She smirked at me.

"Now, I want you to think of your world..."

She held up the clear sphere.

"...like this."

She waved her hand once more, creating another sphere this one was blue.

"This one will represent our world. They are completely separate but..."

She took both spheres, and pushed them together. The clear one covering the blue one. You could see the blue one was completely inside of the clear sphere.

"Your world was created around ours. Or it pushed itself away from ours we aren't entirely sure. It seems more like 'time' made a copy of our world and pushed them away from the earth, while still remaining attached to it. Look at the veil again tell me what you see now."

Helena instructed me calmly.

I looked back at the cloak type structure, and suddenly it was like one of those optical illusions. You know the one that look like a vase at first, but after you stare at it long enough you see two silhouette of faces looking at each other. It was like my brain couldn't see what was truly in front of me at first. Once I understood it better my brain allowed me to see it more clearly.

"That is so strange. At first it was as if it was just on the horizon. But now that I looked closer, it was as if it was above me. Like it was floating in the air. Is that what you see?"

I asked dumbfounded.

"I guess you could say it like that. Though they are not truly floating in the air. It looks as if they are just out of reach, but technically they are in their own dimension. We can see it. Your people can not."

Helena shook her head at that thought.

"It seems to be on the edge of our atmosphere. It looks closer than it truly is. This is really hard to explain. I feel as if I am making this much more difficult than it is."

She stopped I think to ponder to herself.

"It is like trying to explain what

a tomato tastes like if someone has never had one."

I said remembering how Christian had said that to me.

"Yes that is exactly what it is like, thank you. That sums it up perfectly."

She smiled at me.

Chapter Forty One

"Well, Helena, I believe that you are doing a fine job."

Evangeline said.

"Maybe you both should look at it like the Aperture. It is always around, we just have to acknowledge its presence?"

Evangeline chimed in.

"That is a very good explanation. Thank you. Yes it is always around, but not until you open your mind to it do you see it."

Helena mused.

"So how did you keep others from viewing or going through the veil if it is everywhere? And how was I sucked in and others weren't if it is all around us"

I asked curiously.

"We trust. Trust that they

won't disobey our laws. It's not really enforced per say unless caught doing the crime. As for what happened to you, and why others haven't been pulled through. I guess you could say that while you are viewing the veil you are essentially between the realms. So you were technically in between the two realms not completely in either of the realms."

She informed me.

"Oh I see. So Christian wasn't in this realm when he was looking through the veil."

I said in understanding.

"Yes that is correct. When you are merely viewing the other realm you are in the 'Amid' as we call it. Or as you might say the in between."

Helena informed me.

"So when I was pulled within the creation of 'times' clutches I was in the as you call it the 'Amid'. So I was in between the two realms and got trapped on the other side."

I think I have a better understanding now. This makes me feel more at ease.

"So you said you use to go between the realms. How did that work? I understand that it's different now but I want to know how it use to work."

I said hoping that I didn't sound completely stupid. It was Evangeline who answered my question.

"It was similar to how we travel now. We would part the air like we do to create the Aperture, but instead of the Aperture we created a sort of gap. A gap like when you push a curtain aside. We entered through the gap in 'time'. We would pass through the curtain and we would find ourselves in the 'Amid'. From there we would just simply float down to our realm. As to how we got there it was as simple as thinking it."

Evangeline gave me a quick smile.

"You are in a sense transported with your thoughts to the nothingness that is the 'Amid'. It's not as if there is a stairway or a door that you can climb or walk though. You are taken there by your own will. Have I helped you any?"

Evangeline asked me.

"That actually makes sense to me. Thank you both for putting up with me. I know I have been asking a lot of really dumb questions, but this is all so weird to me."

I smiled at them both.

This was it, there was nothing holding me back now. I understood more about myself and how this side of the veil worked. Knowing what was at stake. and how many people were trapped, I needed to return to help set things right.

"I think I am ready now. Thank you for your help. I hope to see you both again soon. I will try and send as many lost souls back as I can before I attempt to return myself. Will you help those who cross just as you have with me?"

I questioned them.

"Yes we will."

They both said in unison. Together they came to me and gave me a warm hug. Wishing me well.

"Hold on to your lessons, practice what we have taught you. We will be here when you return."

Helena said to me. I just hoped that she was right about me returning. I turned my attention back to the veil. I closed my eyes and thought to myself how I would like to go there. When I opened my eyes again I was in the 'Amid' as they called it. I was surrounded by nothing. My body was just hovering there in the air. As far as I could see there was zilch. It was just as Evangeline said. I parted the veil to form a gap in 'time'. Just before crossing the veil I closed my eyes and telepathically reached out to Christian.

"I love you, wish me luck. I will be with you soon, stay hopeful."

"As I you my love. Remember what I vowed to you. If you are not through the veil again before my sentencing is through I will come to find you."

Christian told me telepathically.

With his vow ringing in my head I crossed through the gap in 'time'. I returned to the realm I had been trapped in for as long as I could remember. The only life I could remember.

Chapter Forty Two

Once I emerged through the gap in 'time' I was engulfed with a massive headache. At first I was paralyzed with the pain. Unable to concentrate on my surroundings. Helena's words came flooding to the front of my mind.

"You can heal any injury."

I was capable of changing or fixing anything in my body. I told this to myself, taking a deep cleansing breath. Squeezing my eyes shut tighter I focused on the pain. Looking for where the pain was located in my brain. Once I found the place in which the pain was radiating I concentrated on how to correct the problem. Once I released the pressure I was able to open my eyes. The pain that had so suddenly attacked me was now a dull throb.

Looking around I had a strange

feeling that something was different. I just couldn't quite grasp what it was. I need to get a game plan. First I needed to see what had been happening while I had been away. While trying not to get sucked back into the concept of 'time'. I must remind myself it wasn't real. I went back to my apartment and rang the buzzer.

"Hello?"

Came a male's voice through the intercom that I didn't recognize. Crap what do I say?

"Umm, I'm sorry, I'm looking for Paige, or Emily?"

I said. Shit maybe I should have used their last names.

"I'm sorry you must have the wrong address."

He said through the intercom.

"Oh I'm sorry to have bothered you."

I said through the intercom. Well, I wondered where I should go next. Thinking to myself how long I had been gone. I had no idea how quickly things could change on this side of the veil. I could have been gone for months, or years. The thought popped into my head that there was a possibility that everyone that I knew was already gone. Well passed into another life. I had never even thought about that.

After a moment of quiet contemplation I decided that I needed to see for myself. I decided to walk the seven blocks to my family home. I needed to figure out what had happened since I left this realm. Even though it was a short walk I went slowly.

I tried to take all that I could in. As I was walking I felt as though I was being watched. It was as if every person that I walked by was looking at me as if I was wearing a tin foil hat or something completely bizarre. I started to feel self-conscious.

I stopped in front of the newspaper box. I needed to know what was happening. When it was, and how long I had been gone from this realm. I looked at the date. My mouth dropped open as I realized to the timelings how long it had been sense I had left.

This was going to be extremely hard to explain. I thought to myself as I just stood there holding the paper, with my mouth to the ground.

"I can't go home."

I could barely whisper. This was all too much. There was no way I could explain any of this. I just didn't know what I should do. I needed to just get my bearings. Feeling completely lost I felt that sensation again that the world was starting to spin, and that deep ringing was starting to take over my hearing. The pain was back in full force. The temporary throb was now back to its original sharp stabbing pain. I tried to push it out again, but it was different somehow. The next thing that I knew, I was surrounded by feet, and people whispering. That's when it all went black.

When I came to there was a steady beeping noise, and the air smelled like disinfectant. I opened my eyes slowly as if I was afraid to see where I was. When I looked around the room that I was in, I saw a TV hanging on the white wall. There was a large window with metal blinds. Next to me was a chair, and several monitors. Well that explained the constant beeping. I was lying in a bed with guard rails and a call button was draped over the side of the railing. Crap I must have fainted and was taken to the hospital. Double crap.

Chapter Forty Three

This couldn't be good. What was I going to do? I started to wonder if they knew who I was. I thought back, was I carrying my wallet with me when I first walked to the park, before I jumped into the other realm?

Yeah, I remembered grabbing it just in case I wanted to stop for a coffee before going back to the apartment. So they must know who I was. Just as I was having a debate with myself whether I should stay and let things play out, or jump out of this bed and make a run for it. A nurse came into the room to check on me. I guess that question had been answered for me for the moment. She was a tall young women, with burgundy hair that cut off just above her shoulders.

"Oh good, your awake. My name is Izzy, I'll be your RN for the next eight hours. Your Doctor is Dr. Fields she will be glad to hear that you are finally awake. I have some questions for you. Do you feel up for that just yet?"

She asked with a hopeful tone.

"Yeah, sure. What would you like to know?"

I said back to her.

"Do you know what your name is, and where you are?"

Izzy asked me calmly.

"My name is Rosalie White, and I'm in the Bowdle Hospital in South Dakota I presume."

"Yes, and do you know what happened?"

She asked me.

"I had panic attack, I guess that is what the doctor will probably call it."

I said feeling stupid. I wondered why they brought me to the hospital for passing out. I mean I know I had been doing this a lot recently. That was completely understandable, for all the mind blowing information I have had to endure. Well they didn't know that I had been doing this. I was sure as hell not going to tell them either. They would probably poke and prod me with needles, till I looked like a pin cushion. I thought to myself.

"So, you had a panic attack? That's what you think caused your fall? Have you had a panic attack before?"

She questioned me as she was scribbling something down in my chart.

"No... not really."

I lied.

"Why do you think you were having a panic attack? What do you think caused you to go into the attack?"

She asked me with a curious tone of voice.

Crap I didn't think that through. What was I going to tell them? I most definitely couldn't tell them I panicked when I saw the date. Stating that I hadn't been in this realm in ten years. Also that I freaked out when I couldn't think about what I was going to make up for the reason I disappeared. Where I had been. What I had been doing. I think I was going to play it stupid.

"I don't know I just felt my

heart racing. Then there was a ringing in my ears, and I had a massive headache. That was the last thing that I remember."

"Do you know what day it is?"

She asked me as she scribbled some more notes in the chart.

Crap. What did the newspaper say? I needed to try not to get sucked back into the belief of 'time'. I didn't know what would happen if I started to use the terms again. Could I start to forget just because I went along with them so that they didn't suspect me of being crazy?

"Umm... Saturday?"

I said.

"The date?"

She prompted.

"No, I don't remember. I am horrible with dates."

I said in a tactic to avoid further prompting.

"The month?"

She asked.

Umm the paper said it was August. Well at least I think it said August.

"August?"

I said.

"Ok, Rosalie you are doing great. Dr. Fields will be in shortly to see you. If you need anything just hit the buzzer and I will be right with you ok."

She said in a calm voice.

"Sure that's fine."

I said to reassure her that I was ok. Man why was she acting like this was such a big deal? I didn't think I bashed my head on anything when I fell. She was acting really weird. I wondered if it has something to do with the fact that I had just up and disappeared for "ten years".

When I looked up someone walked into the room.

Chapter Forty Four

"Hello Miss. White. How are you feeling?"

Doctor Fields, asked me. She was a short petite woman with red frizzy curls. She had on a dark grey pants suit and a turquoise blouse covered with a white lab coat the doctors wore.

I'm good thank you, so could I be discharged now?"

I asked hopefully.

"Rosalie, I'm afraid there is something you haven't been informed about yet."

"Informed about what?"

I asked.

"Did anyone tell you how long you have been unconscious?"

She queried.

"No. Should they have?"

I asked while I was thinking

how much I didn't care about their concept of 'time'. I needed to get out of this place before I got trapped once again by the creation.

For all I knew 'time' was coming for me. I shuddered at the thought. If this lady kept questioning me like this it was going to get really difficult. I wouldn't be able to keep evading the concept of 'time'.

"I understand why they haven't told you anything just yet. They were probably afraid to frighten you considering your fragile state."

She said to me.

"What the hell does that mean? Just because I passed out that means I am in a fragile state?"

I snapped at her.

"No Rosalie. You didn't just pass out, you have been in a coma for the past eight months."

If I believed in the concept of time, I probably would have shouted what? How is that possible? But for me I had just passed out and woke up. I may be in their realm, but I am not affected by their 'time'. I needed to be careful to keep it that way.

"Rosalie... do you have any feelings about what I just told you?"

She asked me in a resurging voice.

"Well, what do you think caused that?"

I asked her hoping that she would give me some ideas to work off of. Give me something to explain some of my other problems. Like what happened while I haven't been in this realm.

"Rosalie, over the past eight months I have been doing some tests. During those tests I have noticed that your brain activity is quite strange. Along with some swelling in your brain. I would like to do some more tests now that you are conscious."

She paused momentarily to look at my chart.

"I would like to get to the bottom of this. We wouldn't want this to happen again. This could be a serious condition. If not treated you could be risking your life or the lives of others. What would have happened if this had happened while you were behind the wheel of a motor vehicle? I say this not to frighten you but to help you to understand why I am not ready to release you just yet. I would really like to get to the bottom of this."

She said with an authoritative voice. Not really giving me a choice at all.

"Yes I can see where you are coming from."

I said.

"Also the police would like to speak with you. About your whereabouts for the last ten years."

She stated that in matter of fact. While she was giving me this look. Oh I hated this woman. She was one of those women who thought just because she was a doctor that she was better than everyone else. Well only if you knew what I was capable of lady.

I have half a mind to scream I use more of my brain than you do lady! I don't know why this woman was getting so deeply under my skin. Well maybe I did. I hated those people who thought themselves better than others.

Who cares you went to college and got a degree. I can fly, and talk to others just using my mind.

Well if I screamed that at her they would never let me leave this hospital. Well at least freely. I laughed to myself just as she cut off my internal rant.

Chapter Forty Five

"Rosalie... are you ok? Your blood pressure is starting to spike. Do you feel alright?"

She said as she came closer to me and started to check my vitals. With a concerned look plastered across her snooty face.

I closed my eyes and told my body to slow down. I forced my heart to beat slower and my body listened. I need to be very careful while I was hooked up to all these machines. When I opened my eyes Dr. Fields was over next to the machine that was spitting out paper. She was looking at the last couple of lines and marking them with a pen. When I looked back up she was giving me this look. I couldn't place what emotion was going through her at that moment, but I feared that it wasn't a good one. Well at least not one for me to be getting released.

"Well Rosalie I want to keep you hooked up to these monitors just a little longer. I will have your nurse come and take out your catheter. After that I am sure the police will be in to see you, and ask their questions. Alright, I will be making my rounds now but I will be back in the next hour to check on you. If you need anything please use the call button, and a nurse will be in to help you."

That's when she took her leave of my room and shut the door. Just as I was about to release the breath that I had been holding, since the good Doctor was scrutinizing me with her cold eyes. My nurse Izzy came bustling into the room with a cheerful whistle, and an infectious smile.

"Hey there sleeping beauty. I hear you are ready to get that catheter out."

She said in an overly perky voice. I thought to myself how I instantly liked her.

"Yeah that would be great."

I smiled back at her.

After the catheter was out Izzy told me that the Detectives were waiting just outside the door for me.

"If you need anything at all just push the button ok hun."

"Actually I could use some food. Apparently it's been a while since I've had a good meal."

I laughed.

"I will see what Dr. Fields has approved for you dietary needs ok. We wouldn't want to over whelm your system after going so long without solid foods. It might just be Jell-O and stuff for at least another day or two. Do you have a favorite flavor?"

Izzy asked me with a cheerful grin.

"Yeah could I have some strawberry? I hate lime and cherry with a passion so none of those please."

"Sure thing hun. I will see what I can do."

As she walked out of the room the two Detectives came in.

"Hello Miss. White. My name is Detective Marks, and this is my partner Detective Samuelson. We have a few questions for you, if you feel up to answering them?"

He said. But I didn't think it really mattered if I felt up to answering them or not. They wanted answers.

"Umm yeah sure I can try. What would you like to know?"

I asked as innocent sounding as I could. Maybe I could play dumb, or the, I've been in a coma plea. For me it was moments, for them it was months. Well let's see how far I could push this. I looked at the two gentlemen before me. Marks was tall with a lean figure. His face was showing signs of aging with wrinkles around his eyes and forehead. While Samuelson was a heavier set man with a younger complexion than his partner.

"Well first off we want to know where you have been for the last ten years. Were you held against your will? Or did you just decide you wanted to leave of your own free will?"

Detective Marks asked me with a scrutinizing look across his face, which made his wrinkles deepen in his forehead.

What should I say? If I told them I just left their going to ask why I didn't tell anyone anything. If I say that I was taken they'd want details. They would want descriptions of my assailants.

Chapter Forty Six

"It's kind of foggy."

I said hopping playing dumb could help. I needed to sell this. Also not giving them too much to go on.

"What do you mean by foggy?"

Detective Samuelson asked in a probing way.

"The last thing I really remember is trying to walk to my parent's house."

I said in a timid voice.

"So you have no recollection of where you've been for the last ten years?"

Detective Marks asked me sounding skeptical. Like he didn't believe a word that was coming out of my mouth.

"I remember being in the park. I had walked there from my

apartment that I had with my two best friends. We were just unpacking when I decided to call it quits. I wanted to go somewhere where I could sit, while thinking about some life decisions. Like what classes I needed to sign up for. Then it's a big foggy. More of a big blank."

I said. Taking a deep breath I went on.

"The next thing I remember is walking to the apartment. I buzzed the intercom because I couldn't find my keys. Some guy came on and said he didn't know my friends. So I started to walk to my parent's house. When I saw the newspaper and I must have passed out, and that's when I woke up here."

I said as I motioned with my hands for emphases.

"Now they tell me that I have been here for oh I don't even remember what she said. I take it it's been awhile?"

I said trying to pull of the damsel in distress look.

"Where are my parents? Do they know that I am here? Have they been here to see me?"

I asked them. Not just because I was trying to play the victim card, but I was also curious. Just because I knew they weren't my family, not really but they still meant the world to me. I still loved them.

Marks and Samuelson looked back and forth from one another. What was going on? Why did they have that look on their faces? I was going through all the different scenarios that could possibly be the reason for those looks. When it hit me like a bomb. The reason they weren't here. The reason they were afraid to talk to me about them. It was because they were dead.

"I am sorry to have to tell you this Miss. White, but your parents were in an accident eight months ago. They were on their way to the hospital to see you when, a truck jacked knifed on the interstate and went into a roll. They were killed on impact of the truck. I am sorry for your loss."

Detective Marks said. In a sorrowful tone.

"I...I... I see."

I said grief-stricken. They may not have truly been my parents, but they were all I ever knew. I grew up with the belief that I was their child. They taught me everything. They cared for me and loved me. I knew they weren't really gone, but I would never see them as they were again. They would be, or already have been born into another life. Starting anew all over again, and again unless I helped them out of this never ending cycle. I don't know how I was going to do it just yet.

I wouldn't stop till I found a way to right the wrongs of some men. Men that thought they were creating something helpful, but instead they ended up trapping a countless number of lives within an endless loop of pain and suffering. Where they believed in loss and were unable to help themselves break free from their captivity.

Chapter Forty Seven

"Miss. White. Are you ok? Would you like me to get you your nurse? Miss. White?"

I heard Detective Marks asking. I just couldn't find the words to answer him. It was as if my mouth had forgotten how to move. They're gone. It's all my fault. They were coming to see me. If I hadn't disappeared they wouldn't have been in the accident. I didn't know how I should feel. They were my parents, well at least I had always thought of them as my parents. But really they were just trapped souls that have been reincarnated over and over again. Reincarnated souls that believed the cycle of life involved creating life by having children. A child they perceived as me. The fact that in another life I could have been their parent or best friend. A lover or a teacher. The possibilities were endless.

I technically had no relation to them. It felt wrong not to mourn them as my parents though. I needed to find a happy medium here. I needed to mourn the loss of my family as they were a part of my life. Well at least Rosalie Whites life. When I finally looked up from my internal thoughts Izzy was standing next to me. She had her one hand gently rubbing my back.

"Rosalie, honey, are you alright?"

"Yeah, I just need some space to think."

I said still in a trance like state.

"It's alright honey, you take all the time you need."

She turned to the two Detectives and said in a hushed voice.

"She has had a lot to process in such a short time. She needs some time to recuperate and think things through. If you would like you can leave a card for her to call you back or you can come back a different day."

Izzy said with such authority even though she was speaking so quietly so not to disturb me.

"Umm... but we still haven't found out where she has been for the last ten years. We need to know if someone took her or if she left on her own..."

He was cut of abruptly when Izzy interrupted him with saying.

"Well you will have to wait for the answers to those questions, as she is in no state to answer those questions at the time being. So out you go!"

She said as she pushed them from my room. She came back in with a tray.

"Dr. Fields still wants you on a semi liquid diet until tomorrow. I got you two strawberry Jell-O's, and some applesauce. What would you like to drink?"

She asked me in a soft tone.

"Water will be fine thank you."

I said still looking straight ahead at the wall.

"I will be right back with a fresh pitcher of water. If you need anything else just let me know ok."

She said as she picked up the pitcher and headed out the door once more.

I picked up the Jell-O and gobbled it up. Even though apple sauce wasn't really my thing I was going to suck it up just this once. When I was finished I sat there trying to think about how I was going to convince others that 'time' wasn't real. I was trying to sift through different ideas of how I should do this. When my head started to throb again.

Monitors started to beep and alarms started to go off. All of it making my head hurt even worse. I doubled over in pain. Again I felt the tell tale signs that I was going to pass out. Just before it all went black I saw Izzy run into the room.

Chapter Forty Eight

I could hear what was going on, but was unable to move. I was unable to tell them anything.

Doctor Fields was shouting orders around the room.

"I need a CT scan. Izzy what happened?"

She practically shouted.

"I'm sorry Dr. Fields I wasn't in the room until after the alarms were sounding."

She said. As I saw a bright light flashing into my eyes. That was when the pain over took me and I was unable to keep my attention on the circus that was going on around me. The pain was almost unbearable, it felt as if my brain was about to explode. I tried to take slow deep breaths. Each time I attempted to take in a breath, the pain increased. The ringing in my years took over. It got louder and louder.

I tried to make the pain go away like I had before. This was different than before at the veil. It was as if something was attacking me. Targeting specific areas in my brain, to render me helpless. What could be the cause of the pain? I wasn't injured. How could I heal what's hurting if I couldn't focus on where it was coming from?

That's when realization hit me. There wasn't something wrong with my body. My brain was under attack from an outside force trying to break through my defenses. The sounds I was hearing were there to confuse me into thinking I was going to pass out. It was like something was trying to trigger something inside of me to make me go unconscious.

I needed to fight. I couldn't let something take control. What was I going to do? I needed to act now, stopping whatever it was that was trying to break into my mind before it had the chance to do any harm.

I put all my energy into pushing the pain out wards. Now that I understood that the pain wasn't coming from within, I didn't need to focus on where the pain was coming from. I didn't need to figure out how to heal anything, as nothing was hurt. In a way it became easier. I knew that something was trying to, I guess you could say break into my mind. So I decided that I needed to create a wall. Put up a force field of sorts. I wasn't going down without a fight.

Suddenly the ringing started to subside. The pain started to recede. Once the pain was in the manageable parameters again, I became mindful of my surroundings. It was dark. The air still smelled of sanitizer, and there was a gentle beeping to my right. I opened my eyes. I was still in the hospital but it looked to be a different room. I felt around for my call button. Once I located it I hit the red button.

Suddenly there were three people who came running into my room. They all started to look at my monitors in a frenzy. The one was Dr. Fields. She started to ask me a bunch of questions as she looked me over.

"Rosalie, do you remember where you are? Do you remember what happened? How are you feeling now?"

She asked me in a rushed tone.

"Yes Dr. Fields. I remember that I am in the hospital after I had a fall. I was talking to the Detectives when I woke. After the deceives left, my head started to hurt. I had a loud ringing in my ears, the pain in my head started to hurt really bad that's when I blacked out. I feel better now though."

I said.

"That's very good news. I am glad to hear that you feel better now. Do you know how long you were out this time?"

She asked me.

"No."

I said, I really wish she would stop quoting 'time'. I knew that she didn't understand. It was just that I was still new to this and I didn't want to get sucked back in. I knew I needed to play along for a little while.

"Rosalie, you've been out for four months."

"Oh, I see. What is causing me to black out?"

I asked hopping that she would stop staring at me like, I might slip back into a coma like state at any moment.

Chapter Forty Nine

"That is what I would like to find out. This time I'm not taking any chances. We are going to get you in for a CT scan right now."

As she said that the other two people who had rushed into the room with her were unhooking some cords and preparing my bed for transportation.

"I have gotten many scans of your brain while you have been in your coma like state, but I want to see what is going on while you are fully awake."

We were now on the move. They rolled my bed down the long hall and into the waiting elevator.

The two I guess nurses were talking to Dr. Fields about contrast and images. When I tuned them out. I needed to talk to Christian. I placed my hand over the locket he had given me. I wanted to hold it for some form of comfort. I closed my eyes and just as I was about to reach out to Christian Dr. Fields broke my concentration, by taking my hand and feeling for my pulse.

"Rosalie, Rosalie are you going into one of your attacks? Are you ok? Are you still with us?"

There was a hint of panic and an underlining tone of frustration in her voice. I broke from my thoughts of reaching Christian. I assured Dr. Fields that I was fine, that I was just closing my eyes to try and clear my busy thoughts. She nodded in understanding, and from the looks of it a sigh of relief.

We made it to the CT room. It was a large room with only the CT machine and a sectioned off area for the tech to stand during the procedure. The walls had a few scattered pictures on them but other than that, there wasn't much to look at. I figured that my communicating with Christian would have to be done when I wasn't being watched like a hawk.

After they were done with the CT scan I was taken back to my room where I swear they took half of my blood, to run some tests on.

Finally they left me alone. I closed my eyes and took in calming deep breaths. I used my mind to search for the other half of my soul.

"Christian..."

As I call for him with my mind, the pain found a break in my defenses. The pressure kept finding pathways that lead deeper into my head. I used my hands to hold my throbbing cranium. What is this? I changed my focus from trying to reach Christian to fighting the intruder that had invaded my mind. At this point it was harder to push the intruder from my head. It was harder than it was for me before. It took all of my concentration, to expel the invader from the depths of my mind.

This had to be a force that was intuitive. Calculating. It seemed to be foiling my attacks as I was trying to push it one way, it maneuvered in another direction. It was finding paths that lead deeper into the depths of my thoughts. I used all of the energy that I had to think steps ahead of the trespasser. It was like an intense game of chess. I created mental barriers to keep the invader at bay. I made the barriers around my most precious memories.

Ones that if lost I would never be able to find my way back. My way back to my soulmate, my other half. Once I put up the barriers I went on the attack. I assaulted the pressure with force. I took no prisoners. It was pure furry that fueled my madness. My mind was getting weaker but still I pushed on. I forced myself to keep going. Till finally I got the unwelcome entity from my body. I had used all of the reserves of energy that I had. After that I collapsed into the bed further and slept.

Chapter Fifty

I n my dreams I saw people, people that I didn't know how but I knew them. I couldn't remember their names but their faces were so familiar. I just couldn't place from where.

My dreams started in the clouds. We were having fun, laughing and enjoying each other. The dream shifted to a weird place. People wearing strange clothing and were looking tired.

They were very interesting. I enjoyed watching them. They created funny objects. Things that they thought to be useful items. This made me laugh. They were funny because the objects made things so much more difficult than it should be. They didn't use their magic. Everything they did was so silly. I liked watching them, they made me laugh.

The people began to look sad,

wiry even. Their skin started to wrinkle, and sag. Their hair started to turn different colors and fall out. They began to hunch over as if they could no longer hold up their changing frail looking bodies. All of a sudden some of the people collapsed. The others dug holes in the ground and placed the fallen bodies with in them. I gasped feeling mortified. Shocked. What were they doing? I tried to get a closer look, but changed my mind and continued to just keep watch from my cloud.

Some of the people who looked healthier became excited when their wives stomachs became swollen. Once the women looked as if they would explode they pushed out a small human. This was interesting. They made mini humans and called them babies. These babies as they called them began to grow into larger humans like their creators, which they called parents. This became a cycle for them they called it aging. As they aged they died, and were reborn as babies. As this went cycle after cycle, the people seemed to become fractured. Shattered pieces of their former selves. I couldn't stand to watch any longer.

I wanted to help. I wanted to tell them that they didn't need to live in their never ending cycle. As I tried to intervene a hand grabbed my arm. I turned to face the person who had a hold of me. It was my soulmate. My other half. He was fearful of that place. He stopped me from proceeding. His eyes told me he was afraid that something would happen to me if I confronted them.

"Don't go."

He begged.

"I'm afraid, I don't want anything to happen to you."

He said with worry stricken across his face.

That face I knew it. My heart longed to reach out and stroke the worry of his soft but strong features. His eyes were always my undoing. I could stare at them forever. Suddenly I felt a pulling force from behind me. When I looked to see who was grabbing me, there was no one there.

It was as if there was a rope around my waist. It pulled me until I was within the other world in which I had been watching. Pain invaded my mind. I collapsed to my knees. I screamed out in pain.

Begging for it to stop. Pleading for anyone... someone to help me.

There was a deep ringing that took over my hearing. I was no longer able to see. The pain was shutting down all of my senses one by one. I tried to heal my body of the pain in which I was in. Just as I had always done whenever I was hurt, or in pain from something. Every part of my body that I tried to heal became taken over by something. I didn't understand it. My body was no longer listening to my commands. I was unable to heal myself as I had always done. Finally I just gave in to the pain. As I was unable to solve this mystery with in my mind. I just let go.

After I stopped fighting the pain seemed to lessen but I still could not control my body. I had become a shell. A prisoner within myself. The thing that had taken over me continued to roam around my body. Making changes here and there. Mostly it worked within my brain. It started to section off parts of my mind. After they were sectioned off I was unable to reach those areas. The sectioned off areas were blocked by some form of a barrier. I tried to remember what was behind the barriers. I became frustrated trying to remember what it was that I couldn't remember. I had just known what was there. In a instant it was gone.

I couldn't remember why I was trying so hard to break the barriers. Finally I decided that the barriers were nothing important. Until finally I decided to just leave them alone altogether. Once I did that I began to regain the use of parts of my body that had been taken over. I became less afraid, and little by little I got the operation of my body again. I stretched out. It felt good to move around. I couldn't remember how I had gotten here, who I was, or what I had been doing before the pain had started.

I started to look around. I found a group of people in a small village. They took me in and offered me food and a place to sleep. I couldn't remember my name so they helped me chose one. I became Caroline. Caroline Wilson. I took on my new Family's last name as I adapted to their lifestyle. I had completely forgotten how I had come to be in this place. Furthermore I couldn't have cared less, why or how it had happened. I didn't have a feeling of loss or foreboding. I felt one with the people who were so kind to help me when I was lost. Along with not remembering who or where I was before I had come to this place.

They allowed me to stay with them so long as I used my time to help out around the house. In addition with helping with the care of the children. I became a live in maid and care giver to the children of the Wilson family. As the days passed I felt that there was something missing in my life. I began to wonder if in my short life if I would be lucky to find love like the Wilsons. The couple who had been so kind to take a stranger in, and welcome her into their family.

Life is so short, I must not waste it with silly things such as daydreaming of an imaginary man whom I see in my dreams. A man with a glorious body, light brown hair and beautiful blue eyes. Eyes that call to the depths of my soul. Calling for me to come to him as he is on his knees crying for his Victoria to come back to him. I didn't know why my subconscious chose the name Victoria. Maybe Caroline was just too simple a name for my dream gentleman to desire. I didn't know why my dream gentlemen would want to be with a simple brunette with light brown eyes like myself. A man like that deserved to be with a blonde blue eyed beauty that had lavish skin. Though he made me feel like a princess, the way he looked at me. If only he was real, and not imaginary.

Chapter Fifty One

I knew that I was dreaming, but I was just so tired from my struggle. The struggle with the unknown trespasser. The dreams were a very interesting way to just relax. I watched Caroline as she grew older. It was as if I was just along for the ride. I watched as she searched, looked for someone to love. Someone to love her. I couldn't do anything but watch her life as it flew by.

She started to travel after the duty of watching the children was over. The Wilson children had all grown and moved on with their lives. Caroline started to travel in her search to find what her soul seemed to be longing for, trying to find what it was pleading for her to find. Even though she wasn't sure what it was. As she aged she searched for someone who could make her feel, whole, complete.

She never found him. She died with a broken heart at age seventy two. Her heart couldn't bear the loneliness any longer. I was sad for her, but she was reborn after spending what felt like a short while in a foggy area. There was nothing but what seemed like a mist, or a haze. Her soul seemed to float around in the nothingness till it was pulled into a new being.

When a new being, or a baby as they called them was born she inhabited that vessel. Taking me along with her to her new body, her new life. She was a blonde green eyed little girl born into a wealthy family. They named her Kathrine Smith. Though she had no memories of her past self, she was like Caroline in many ways.

I could see that Kathrine was a kind child, but was spirited in many ways. She loved to explore the grounds of her family's land in England. She would go to the stables and watch the help grooming the horses. Even though her parents disapproved of her spending her time watching the help. Her parents believed they were lesser people, filthy beings who didn't deserve the time of day. If they were pore they were nothing. Not Kathrine, she loved each and every one of them, they were kind to her as she was to them. She never treated them like they were any less than she was herself. Why should she after all? It wasn't like we got to choose whom our parent were. She enjoyed doing things that her parents disapproved of. It gave her a thrill to do the things in which they were displeased with.

She married a wealthy man that her parents suited her with. Not for love but because it was how things were done in wealthy families in that day and age. He was a handsome man, and he was rich to boot. Kathrine was still unhappy.

Even though she got to travel and see the country side with her rich handsome husband. He was more like her parents than she would have liked. Though she learned to live with him as he was. She felt like something was missing in her life. She wanted more, but she didn't know what more was. She felt a hole that reached all the way into her soul.

She spent money trying to fill the void in her soul with objects. When that didn't help she had babies. Nothing seemed to fulfill the emptiness that seemed to consume her. She loved her husband and children, but she couldn't understand why a life so full was yet so empty. Kathrin lived to be eighty, still wanting more, till the day she died from smallpox. Kathrin suffered from smallpox till the fever overcame her blistered covered body.

Kathrine was reborn to a pore family. After only spending moments in the empty void. They named her Julia Powell. Again remembering nothing from her lives before. I moved on with Julia as she grew. She was kind down to the last black hair on her head.

Even though her and her family were poor they were rich with loving family and friends. They lived in a small cottage. Julia was the eldest of five children. She was always helping her mother taking care of the younger children, and helping around the house. Julia always had something to do, or someone to take care of. Even though she was always busy she too felt that there was something missing in her life. She was always searching for someone to love. A love like her parents had found. She was beautiful with thick flowing straight black hair, tan skin and lovely brown eyes. Even though she was stunning she lived her life as a single woman. Never finding one to fill her heart with the kind of love she saw her parents had. It wasn't from lack of interest on the part of her suitors. She had many men who tried to appeal to the dark haired beauty. But Julia gave them no never mind. She hadn't felt the connection she was longing for. So she spent the time with the things that she enjoyed doing which was helping others in any way that she could.

She became a nurse, so she could put her love of helping others to good use. She chose to be one of the travelers to the new world. As they were in need of nurses on the long voyage. She spent her life helping heal others the best she could. Till the day she became ill treating one of the sick patients that she was caring for. A patient who had become ill with an epidemic of consumption on the voyage to the strange new world. Julia died painfully from the shortness of breath and chronic cough that was filled with her warm blood. Her old lungs couldn't take the infection that ravished her body. She died at age sixty three, never finding what she was seeking, just as her previous selves were also searching for.

Chapter Fifty Two

The cycle continued on. Julia died and was reborn as Helen Mitchel. Helen was an orphan after her mother died in child birth, and her father was killed in a work accident before she was even born. She live in the orphanage till she was eighteen, and found a job working as a kitchen aid for a rich family. Helen was stunning with deep sea blue eyes and frizzy blonde curls. She too waited for something to fill the empty hole within her life. She spent her whole life never finding her souls call, and never married. When she died at age seventy one from old age, she was reborn as Judith Moore.

Judith died young from the whooping cough at age fifteen. She was a small frail child. From her birth she was always sick, as she was born a small child. The doctors had always claimed she wouldn't live long. She was too small, too weak to survive any illnesses. It was so sad that she never even had a chance. Her parents fearful for her weak body, that they kept her confined to their family home. She was such a lively child. Always helping others even when she was too small and week to really help. She tried so hard to make her life matter, even at a young age she knew there was something missing. Judith longed to explore the world and go searching for what she knew was missing in her confined life. When she too died. She was reborn into Heather Lewis.

Heather was an independent woman. She never did things just because it was the trend. She was who she was. Damn anyone who tried to change her. She was a thick woman not fat just curvy, with short black hair and hazel eyes. Heathers life came to a tragic end when she was in an unfortunate accident. She was only thirty four when her injuries overcame her and she died. Her injuries were sustained from an overturned carriage, which crushed her. Heather fought for her life as long as she could, without proper care she faded away.

Her soul went into the child that was named Sarah Cromwell. I went along with Sarah and watched her grow into a beautiful women. She was gorgeous with amber hair that caught the sun light in a way that made her face glow. Her eyes were a striking sapphire. When she like her previous selves couldn't find happiness in the world around her, she searched the heavens for the piece that was like an emptiness within her soul.

She devoted herself to God and lived in the monastery. She did all that she could to serve God to the best of her abilities, but still she felt like a piece of her soul was missing. When she died at age ninety one, she too passed on into another life. Sarah died of old age, her body unable to sustain her any longer. Sara was reborn as Elizabeth Malthus.

I knew this was a dream. What else could it be? I watched from one life to another as the soul of Caroline passed down from person to person. I was just watching unable to control my surroundings, or how the dream played out. I was unable to change the events as they unfolded in front of me. I had tried to help when Heather Lewis had been crushed by the carriage. I tried to comfort the small child Judith Moore when she was coughing her last painful breath. It was completely useless. I wasn't able to do anything. I couldn't even talk to them. It was as if I was a ghost. I had no physical form. I had no voice. I was so weak from my physical battle of my mind, I was trapped in this what seemed to be never ending dream.

I saw Caroline's soul, now in the body of the child named Elizabeth. The blonde haired green eyed child grew and lived her life in a similar fashion as did the previous host bodies. Yet again death took the soul from her current body, and into another. Her death was caused by the age of 'time". Elizabeth's soul was born into the baby named Carry Grey. When Elizabeth died at age seventy six of a heart attack.

The cycle that had started with Caroline went on and on. I cycled through with the original soul that was Caroline, as we passed through each new host body as time went on. Every time starting fresh with a new name and a different family. They never remembered what had happened in the previous lives.

Till I was taken by surprise when the soul of Caroline traveled from Carry grey, a strange child who had dark brown eyes and a mop of red curly hair, and freckles all over. She died at a young age of twenty. Carry was an unfortunate soul. She was killed by a drunk driver as she was on her way home from work. Her soul went into the child named Rosalie White. I finally realized that this hadn't been a dream. I was reliving my past lies or seeing them for myself. This was the realization that pulled me from my slumber. I was able to wake with my new found strength. I found the strength in the knowledge that my soul never fractured. I was left whole throughout the passing of each life my soul had endured.

I had always known that my soul was missing its other half. My Christian. My true love. Yes I had been married and had children, but they were a small part that never seemed to fit right. Most of my past lives lived searching for him, as he too had searched for me. This knowledge brought a new thought to mind. When I or

Victoria, whatever, was pulled into the veil of 'time', she too had experienced the pain in which I had felt. The pain when I crossed from one realm to the other. That couldn't just be a coincidence. Maybe it was 'time' trying to erase or take control of the person who has crossed.

Helena was right, that 'time' had become aware. It must be trying to stop those who do not have the concept of 'time', from helping those who are trapped within. By stripping the nonbelievers of their memories. Within doing that they were more susceptible to the infiltration of the concept of 'time'.

That's when I opened my eyes and started to scream. I couldn't help myself, it just escaped from my lips.

Chapter Fifty Three

I screamed, which alerted the nursing staff that I was yet again awake. They came flooding into my room trying to find out what had awaken me from what they perceived to bet yet again another coma like state.

They started trying to soothe me with a reassuring tone that I was alright. That I was in a safe place. They were here to help me. That they would not rest till they found the cause of my affliction. That's when my verbal diarrhea kicked in. I was shouting about 'time' coming for me. 'time' was out to erase me as it had before when it pulled me in from my realm, ripping me away from my soulmate. Making me forget who I was and that 'time' doesn't exist. I yelled over and over again that I was fine, that I just needed to get out of this bed.

They were giving me these looks

as if they thought I was crazy. Which made me only want to explain it even more. I tried to tell them that when I died I was reborn into another person. After each death I was reborn into another body, my soul just moved on from one body to another. Up until now I hadn't remembered my previous lives.

That's when they had me transferred to the mental institution. They tried to tell me that my brain was on overload from swelling that accrued from my fall. That was their explanation to why I had been coming in and out of my coma like state. They said I had been in their hospital for the past four years form my initial fall.

They thought that the swelling that was showing in my scans was the reason for why I went into a coma like state and it must be the reason for why I was having delusions of past lives, and felt like 'time' was out to get me. They didn't want to listen to me when I told them that when I was trying to heal myself I was unknowingly showing the creation 'time' the pathways of my brain, allowing it to drain all of my energy, which was what they thought was a coma like state.

They chalked everything down to a breakdown of my brain capacity from the swelling. They couldn't see that it wasn't swelling, it was me using more of my brain than they ever conceived as a possibility. I wondered if using more of my mind was what alerted 'time' to me. If somehow the creation 'time' could sense me using my full brains capacity. I needed to find a way to break free from this place. I really needed to talk to Christian. I missed him so much. If I couldn't talk to him without alerting 'time' to me, how was I going to reach him?

I became frightened that I might not be able to reach him. That 'time' would keep me trapped in this hospital, attacking me whenever I attempted to use my magic or the full capacity of my mind. First things first. I needed to get out of this mental institution. I couldn't even wait them out. I had found out that the creation 'time' must be altering their views of my appearance.

When I told them to look at me and see that I hadn't been aging while I was in my coma like state, they told me that I had been. Well at least they saw me as aging. Their minds must be controlled by 'time' which was making them see me differently. They believed me to be aging as they themselves were doing.

It must have been "times" way of fixing the situation. Sense it had been unable to mess with my mind it had to result to messing with theirs. With 'time' being unable to erase my memories, it has to put up a front for those who did believe in it. I guess so not to draw suspicion. If I chose to wait for them to pass on into another life, I could see 'time' making them believe I was someone else or, making them forget about me. I can't even begin to fathom how much the creation 'time' had taken control of them. I knew I sound crazy but this was just insane. Pun not intended, sorry.

Chapter Fifty Four

So if trying to communicate alerted 'time' to me I didn't know if I should even try to use my magic. I had all these special abilities and I was stuck in a padded room where people thought I was insane. This was just great.

How was I going to help others break free of "times" clutches if I couldn't even break out of this room? I really needed a plan. Just something that would help me out of this room without alerting 'time' to me. If 'time' came after me there was a chance that it could take over me, as it did when I was pulled in. When I was Victoria.

I knew that it would attack me with a pressure like pain in my brain. It would try to confuse me and make it hard to think with the ringing in my ears. I also knew that trying to heal myself from the pain, would show my adversary the pathways that lead to my thoughts. If that happened it would take control of me and I could be trapped in the endless cycle of dying and being reborn over and over again. If that happened, and I was unable to escape 'time' before Christian's punishment was over he would cross the veil and come searching for me. If that happened he too will be attacked as I was. The thought of him losing his memories and living and dying in this entrapment, made me determined to get free from this cell.

I needed to be smart about this, I needed a really good plan before I attempted anything. Maybe I should try and make them think that I was better. That I didn't believe that 'time' was after me. I doubt that would work. Especially after all they would look to see if the swelling had gone down. So if I was going to try that I would need to find a way to keep them from seeing how much of my brain that I had access to. Even after that they would probably try and keep me in the hospital until they figured out what was the initial cause of my fall. In addition to where I had been the past "ten years" before that.

Maybe I was thinking about all this the wrong way. Just like I had been when I was trying to heal the areas that were in pain. Instead of trying to heal I needed to fight back ignoring the pain. So what if instead of trying to break out, I figured out how to break free of "times" attack. The attack when I accessed the abilities my mind was capable of. That was it. I needed to come up with a way to stop the attack before it happened. Now all I needed to do was figure out how to accomplish that. Then I should be able to get out of here, and reach Christian with my thoughts.

I laid in my bed. The bed within my prison thinking of ways to accomplish my task at hand. I needed an effective way to stop the attack on my mind before it happened. As I was doing this the nurses and Doctors would come and check on me. I just ignored them. I completely blocked them out. I started to think back to when I was attacked. Were it started. I closed my eyes for better concentration. When I figured out where it had started I decided to put a mental barricade there.

It was the same place it started when I was Victoria. Thinking about it, it also tried to pull my focus by taking over my hearing with a low tone. Trying to distract me by taking over my sense of hearing. I decided it best to try and cover that line of defense as well. I blocked off my sense of hearing momentarily. If this worked I could open the Aperture to escape to a more secure location. There I could figure out everything else. Once I was free from this imprisonment I could find someplace safe. I could reach out to Christian. Ok so block the pain, and stop it from trying to confuse me with sound. What else might it try?

How could 'time' prevent me from opening the Aperture, and finding a place to hold up till I could get a better sense of what I was dealing with? I thought I should also figure out where I should open the Aperture to. I wouldn't want to get trapped somewhere else and give 'time' a chance to find a way around my defenses.

I couldn't go back until I had at least tried to help the souls who were trapped here. So where else could I go that I would be safe

from 'times' clutches? What gives
it its power? I thought hard about
that.

Chapter Fifty Five

Christian said it was like the creation became strongest once they created things to hold their 'time'. So maybe, it was as simple as the objects in which hold 'time', are part of what powered it. Maybe if I found a place in which there were no objects that held 'time' I would be safe from it. Well, at least for a while. I just needed a place where I could regroup my thoughts. I thought about it.

I needed a place where there wasn't a lot of people either. 'time' was also drawing power or at least the magic from those who believed in it. I had lived in this world or realm for many cycles. I must be able to come up with somewhere that could be a temporary haven. Thinking about safe havens I was drawn back to thoughts of Christian. He always had been my sanctuary. I once again was drawn to the locket which he had given me. I opened the beautiful silver locket. Inside there was the picture of him holding me. Our eyes locked in an embrace that words just couldn't describe. Longing love, bliss. All of them true but not fully capturing the depths of emotion that was flowing between our two souls. I needed to be strong. I must get back to him.

Now that I could remember my past I also remembered what it was like before I became trapped. I remembered my life with Christian when I was Victoria. We were so happy. We lived life like it was an adventure. He would paint the places that we explored. The locket helped give me strength to continue on with my plans. Suddenly a thought came to me in a rush. The painting that I loved so much. The one that was in the reading room. It was a perfect place. Not too many people, and the concept of day and night didn't really follow the rules of 'time' so it could just be enough for me to hide without detection. So if I could manage to prevent 'time' from taking over my mind, while keeping it from preventing the opening of the Aperture, I would open it to Antarctica.

If I was correct Antarctica would be my best chance of avoiding the creation 'time'. So now I thought I was almost ready, for my plan was coming together quite well if I did say so myself. Now I just needed to be ready to do this. What should I do? Should I try to contact Christian again? Or should I pretend to be making my escape to provoke 'time'? This was the last step that I needed to figure out. I didn't want 'time' to figure out that something was up, and try to foil my plans. Man this was really messed up when did I start thinking of 'time' as an entity? Maybe when it attacked me. Hum... that's interesting I didn't even think about it like that till just now. It was like it had become a sentient being.

This could change things. Maybe I needed to make this plan more complex. Make it think I was going to do one thing when I was doing the exact opposite. Yes I thought that would be a good plan of attack. After all these people thought that was how magic worked. Make them look this way when their doing something that way. I giggled to myself. This could work.

I lowered my defenses temporally and tuned back into the realm around me. They still had me hooked up to a bunch of monitors. Probably to see if I had another coma like event. Man it was going to be work getting them to believe that 'time' wasn't real, oh well, save that for later. First things first. The nurses had been checking on me often. Without the concept of 'time' being around those who do believe in it seemed to be exhausting. For me a blink of an eye was one of their hours, it seemed.

To them I must have looked like I was catatonic or something along those lines. Maybe if I started to look more active they might get the idea that I was coming around. I started to move around trying to appear normal to them. I tried to smooth back my hair to get a sense of normal. Sure enough a nurse came to my door.

"Rosalie, it looks like you are starting to feel better. Is there anything that I could get for you?"

She said to me in a questioning tone.

"Yes, I would like to see my

doctor. If that would be possible."

I said in a shy voice, trying to seem like I hadn't been myself recently.

"I will go call Dr. Fields for you. Is there anything else you would like?"

She asked me again.

"Maybe some water."

I replied.

"Sure thing."

She said as she walked away from the door.

She came back with my water, and told me that Dr. Fields would be with me shortly. This was it, it was now or never. I unhooked myself from the machines, and waited for them to arrive.

Chapter Fifty Six

When Dr. Fields came to my room I had my mental defenses up. My plan was in motion. When they unlocked the door I was ready to book it. Dr. Fields came into the room with two orderlies. They were both really big men. Not like body builder big, but had an athletic build to them. She must have thought there might be trouble brewing. Maybe because I had unhooked myself from the monitors, or because I was standing there waiting for them. Only if she knew what I really had in mind. She gave me a shy smile, as she started to open her mouth to talk to me. I turned to face the other side of the room. As quickly as I could I opened the Aperture to my selected location, and booked it though allowing it to close just moments after me.

Just before I saw the Aperture

close, I saw the look of shock stream across the Doctors face. It was a moment of pure joy for myself. I had escaped successfully. While I still managed to stick it to the bitch of a doctor, who threw me into the nut house. Ok that's kind of funny. I was the one who was thrown into the nut house instead of Christian. I guess there is still irony in the world. I giggled to myself.

Now for phase two. I needed to create a place where I could practice my magic and get my plan together. Not to mention get out of the blistering cold of the Artic. I decided to wish a small cabin into existence. Closing my eyes I thought of exactly how I wanted it to look. Small but big enough to fit my needs as I was wishing it into existence I decided to wish that it be invisible to those who believe in the creation of 'time'. That way no one could find me that I didn't want finding me. Even though I was literally in solitude, I didn't want 'time' coming after me. I also wished for it to be hidden from the creation known as 'time'. I wished for there to be a dome like barrier to be placed around the cabin. The barrier was to keep anything that believed in 'time' or held 'time' to be kept out.

I walked into the cabin, and set about making myself at home, by creating everything that I would need while I was here. I made a separate room for the living and sleeping areas. In the living room I made a pale green sofa and a white reading chair with black words written on it. I chose to make it a reminder of what I was fighting for. "Free us from our captor, life is more than it seems." Along with a coffee table. And a fuzzy brown rug like Christian had in his house.

Now that I was thinking of it, it was my place too. I smiled for just a moment thinking about Christian. I placed my hand over my locket, pressing it close to my heart. As soon as I got settled I would reach out to him. I promise. I thought to myself. In the bedroom I placed a full sized bed with soft blue satin sheets, and large fluffy pillows within the white room. After I was done with the necessities like a bathroom I decided it best to get my strength up and eat a good meal.

I finally lowered my defenses that I had put into place before my escape. I got to close my eyes with a sense of relief. I took a deep breath and let it out slowly. It felt good to be away from the "Timelings". Great now I was doing it too. I shook my head at the thought. This was it I had made it out of my enclosure. I was safe from the clutches of 'time', well at least for now. I let that thought sink in. It was such a relief to be free form that hospital. There was just something about that place that just didn't feel right from the beginning.

I set about making myself a good meal. Not one with grease or lots of carbs. Nothing like that. I decided that I should treat myself with a healthy meal for once. I magically made a salad, and a bowl of vegetable soup to go along with a generous helping of pot-roast.

Oh how I love magic. I thought to myself as I ate the mouthwatering meal. When I had finally had my fill I used my hands to clear away the mess. I took a seat in the reading chair. Once I had gotten comfortable I used my mind to once again search for Christian.

Chapter Fifty Seven

"*C*hristian... are you there?" I called, not knowing if he could even hear me. Hoped that he could. I hope that the veil of 'time' didn't interfere with our telepathic abilities. I knew that it did before but that could have been because 'time' had sectioned off that part of my mind. Well at least I hoped that was why he couldn't reach me before. Suddenly all those fears vanished like a puff of smoke when I heard him answer my call.

"*Oh Rosalie, I was starting to get worried. I heard you call for me before, but when I had tried to answer you, I felt your pain. I tried to talk to you to see if you were alright, but you didn't respond. I feared that 'time' had taken ahold of you once again.*"

He stopped momentarily for a deep calming breath. I could tell he had been shaken. He had been worried about me. That made me happy to know that he loved me, but hurt me to know that yet again I had brought him pain. This was the man I would do anything to prevent letting harm from coming to him. I wanted nothing more than to reassure him that I was fine. That I was on my way to him. But I still had a job to do. Christian broke me out of my wayward thoughts.

"What happened are you safe? Did you make it back to our side of the veil?"

He asked me with a sense of hopefulness in his tone. I didn't want to shatter his hope but I needed to tell him the truth. I took a deep calming breath before I told him my story.

"I am fine Christian, really but no I have not crossed back to our side of the veil yet."

I stopped momentarily when I heard him gasp. Funny how you can telepathically still gasp I thought to myself. Back to the matter at hand.

"I was in a sense trapped by 'time' but I am safe for now. I promise. I underestimated it. I

promise it will not happen again."

I tried to reassure him.

"I love you so much. I miss you."

I said to him.

"I miss you too my love. Please try and stay safe. I don't know what I would do if anything were too happened to you, while I am stuck here serving my sentencing."

He said with a sad tone.

"I know, but this is important. I need to find a way to save them. Christian I know now that 'time' is in a sense become an entity. It was attacking me in a way that makes me believe that it is capable of thought."

I paused for just a moment before telling him what else has happened to me.

"It has tried more than once to wipe my mind, like it did before. During one of the attacks on my mind it helped to open up my lost memories, and also allowed me to relive, in a sense my reincarnations. The most important of all I remember being Victoria."

He cut me off by gasping again.

"*Really? You truly remember? You don't know how happy that makes me feel.*"

"*Christian...*"

I started, but he cut me off.

"*Rosalie, I don't expect you to just pick up from where we were, when you were Victoria. I understand that you might have mixed feelings about all of this. How are you? Do you want to talk about anything? I am here for you no matter what.*"

"*I love you Christian. I'm sorry... I just can't even begin to think about what my choices are when they come to Victoria. Yes I am her, or she is me... It is just all so confusing to me. Yes I have her memories, but they don't really feel like my own.*"

I was so confused. I couldn't explain the reasoning behind my discomfort. I had the memories not just of my life as Victoria, but I also held the life of Caroline Wilson, Kathrine Smith, Julia Powell, Helena Mitchel, Judith Moore, Heather Lewis, Sarah Cromwell, Elizabeth Malthus, and Carry Grey. Along with the life of the body I now hold. Christian couldn't possibly be ok with me rejecting my life as Victoria. I wasn't even sure myself if I wanted to reject that part of myself.

"I can't even begin to imagine how this could be affecting you. I only want to let you know that I will be here for you in any decisions you make. I love your soul. You are my mate no matter what obstacles that lay before us, we will overcome them my love. Once you have finished your mission, and I have finished with my sentencing we will sit down and continue this conversation face to face. Whatever face that might be."

Christian knew just what to say. His commitment to me throughout all of this has been so amazingly wonderful. He was the most wonderful, kindest, man that has, or would ever walk this earth in my eyes. All I wanted to do was wrap my arms around his neck and never let him go. But for now I couldn't be selfish. I had to do as much as I could to help those that needed my help. I was the only one who was ever going to help them. Helena had said it herself, once I crossed back to our side of the veil there would be no coming back. No I needed to finish my mission. I had to stay strong for now.

Christian, and I talked back and forth with each other. Telling each other what had been happening since we had been apart. I talked to him about what was next to come in my journey, and asked for his input. Christian helped me with my ideas by bouncing around his thoughts with me. He told me how he has settled in, by making a cabin as well. He has been painting pictures of the stars and of me. We finally let each other go with the promise to keep in touch as often as we could. Just knowing that he was just a thought away made it easier to let him go. The next part of my journey might be more complicated. At least I had a safe place to figure out what I was going to do. I also needed to figure out how I was going to proceed. I needed a clear plan to help the souls who were trapped. I had learned from my imprisonment in the hospital that going in unprepared wasn't a smart move. This was a task that was going to need some considerable thought.

After all I was the only one who has ever had to deal with this situation. Now I had to help others believe that 'time' didn't exist. I thought that I was in way over my head here. How do I start? How do

I know who will be willing to listen to me that 'time' was created and has taken over every aspect of their lives. Making them suffer and loose pieces of themselves. It wasn't like I could just go up to complete strangers, and say...

"Hey you may not know me but 'time' doesn't exist. Let me help you cross into another dimension."

That might not go over to well. So I would have to figure out a safe way to save those trapped within this realm, and free them from the creation known as 'time'. Until then I would have to come up with a surefire plan to help them escape.

The end for now...

A Special Preview of

Freed From Time

Book two of

Through the Veil Series.

Chapter One

While I have been in my safe haven I have tried to come up with a plausible plan, to effectively free those who have been trapped by this creation they call 'time'. I now know that 'time' has become in a sense a self-aware entity. A being that is capable of thought. 'time' has trapped the souls of men and women, using their magic, to fuel its own power that it holds over them. I know that just blurting out to strangers that 'time' isn't real won't work. That I would be running the risk of 'time' trapping me once again.

I just can't afford the chance that 'time' will trap me again. I promised Christian that I would be back on our side of the veil before he is done with his sentencing. He is serving his punishment for the crime of viewing through the veil, while he was searching for me. He was sentenced to serve his punishment on Saturn's moon Titan for one orbit around the sun. Though we are separated though the veil of 'time' and space, we are still able to communicate with each other, with the use of telepathy.

I have tried to think of ways to figure out how to get the lost souls to believe me, that 'time' doesn't exist. Along with finding out how to tell between those whose souls are still intact. Or those who either don't have a soul, or have been fractured beyond repair. Not that I have figured out how to repair broken bits of a soul just yet, or if it's even a possibility. It really has been a work in progress. Till finally I came up with the idea to use my magic to help me.

It has become instinct, or a habit whenever I need to calm down or focus. I always grab, or hold tight to the locket that Christian gave me just before Helena sent him away from me. It brings me close to him. Makes me feel like he is there with me. Even though I can talk to him whenever I'd like, it's not the same as having his arms around me.

I closed my eyes concentrating on what I wanted to achieve. While

I held on to the beautiful locket that held within it, the picture of the man who my soul belonged to. The man who risked everything to save me from being trapped within the veil of 'time'. I drew strength from the love that the locket represented. I used that strength and clarity that the locket brought me. It helped me concentrate on what I needed to do. I needed something to help me find and tell the difference between the souls that are whole, or fractured and those who don't have a soul at all.

I wanted something that I would be able to carry around while not drawing attention to me. So that meant that it had to be something small. Maybe something that I could wear that wouldn't draw too much attention. With my mind's eye I watched as I used my magic to fashion a bracelet with a silver band. The band was simple with engravings that swirled around the entire bracelet. I thought about how I wanted to be able to know if someone's soul was whole, fractured, or if they were just an empty shell. I decided that I would use diamonds to help me with this endeavor.

I placed a blue, green, and a clear diamond on the silver band. I told my magic that I wanted the blue diamond to be the indicator that the soul was whole. The green diamond to indicate that the soul has been fractured. While the clear diamond to show that the body held no soul at all. I instructed my magic to make the diamond of corresponding color glow to represent the person I wished to help.

If the blue diamond glowed I would know the person had a soul, therefor I could try and help them. If the diamond glowed green I would need to try and repair their soul before I could attempt to help them. Now the people who made the clear diamond shine I would know that they were empty. That they held no soul within them, and I wouldn't have any way to help them. With no soul they were just empty shells. It saddened me to think like this but my job, or mission is to save those who have been trapped by 'time'. Not those who were created within the realm, that didn't take on a soul that was recycled or reborn.

Once I saw what I wanted my magic to create I used my hands, by swirling my magic in a circle till the object that I had fashioned in my mind was created into a solid form within my hand. When I felt the weight of the bracelet within my hand, I opened my eyes to see what my magic had conjured for me. It was beautiful. The silver bracelet was delicate, with spiral carvings moving freely around it's circumference. The three diamonds were spread evenly at the top of the bracelet. They were in the order blue, green, then clear. The diamonds were each around a caret in size. Each one beautiful, as the light form the cabin hit them they sparkled.

Now that I had a way to tell who I should be trying to help I needed to decide how I was going to brake it to them that what they believed as normal was actually a prison. I put my newly created bracelet around my left wrist, as I moved from the reading chair that I had been sitting in, to pace around the small living room that I had created. As I paced back and forth I started to feel like a pent up animal trapped within a cage. I had been cooped up all by myself in this small cabin since I created it. I missed being around people. Mostly I missed being with Christian. Even though I knew we would be together soon, I still would have liked to be able to be with him at the moment.

I decided my soul needed to hear him. I went into the bedroom and laid down on the full sized bed with the soft blue satin sheets. I laid my head on one of the many large fluffy pillows. That I had placed on the bed within the white room. I reached instinctively to hold the locket once again. I closed my eyes and took a deep breath before I spoke with my mind to the love of my life who was so far away from me.

ABOUT THE AUTHOR

Angela H. Distrola lives in Western New York with her Husband, two children and their dog Jasmin.